I0598306

The Traveller's Companion

A book of over 40 Stories

An assortment of 100-word and other short Stories

by

G, D. Northcott

--oOo--

The Traveller's Companion

Short Stories

G. D. Northcott

 en Press

Copyright © G. D. Northcott 2011

All rights reserved

No part of this publication may be reproduced, stored in a
retrieval system, or transmitted in any form or by any
means, without the prior permission in writing of the
publisher, nor be otherwise circulated in any form of
binding or cover other than that in which it is published and
without a similar condition including this condition being
imposed on the subsequent purchaser.

First published in Great Britain by Pen Press

All paper used in the printing of this book has been made
from wood grown in managed, sustainable forests.

ISBN 978-1-78003-212-2

Printed and bound in the UK
Pen Press is an imprint of
Indepenpress Publishing Limited
25 Eastern Place
Brighton
BN2 1GJ

A catalogue record of this book is available from
the British Library

Cover design Jacqueline Abromeit

*This book of many twists is dedicated to
my Granddaughter, Kristy,
who after reading a few of my earlier stories
compelled me to write a great deal more.*

Contents

100-word Stories:

Other Short Stories:

Continued…

100-word Stories

The Break-in

They had broken in about midnight. It took months of planning. They were professionals. Equipped with a sack-truck for moving the safe and a specially fitted electrical platform to their vehicle enabled the lifting of heavy objects up and into the van.

Not to draw attention to themselves they'd parked in the next street.

John rubbed his hands together like Fagin.

"Full of the weekend's takings," he said with a broad smile.

"Go get the wheels, Ray, and we'll be away."

Ray returned a few minutes later, panting and sweating.

"What's up?"

"Some thieving devil's stolen our van," he snarled.

* * *

High Up

"Don't jump!" she called out anxiously.

He was breathing uneasily but still moved to within one foot of the edge.

"For God's sake, it must be at least 80 feet from the ground," she screamed in a higher pitched voice. A large crowd had gathered and was looking up at him. He glanced down at the people below – he thought he made out two ambulance men in their bright coloured jackets. He moved to just a few inches from the edge now, very determined. She would not try again.

"Alright, have it your own way, do your damned Bungee Jump."

* * *

Unlucky for Some

It was Saturday the 13th. Bob woke up, it was his birthday. He felt lucky. He had only himself to please.

If he went to the racecourse, strangely enough it would be the 13th time there. Bob decided to go.

When inside and looking through the race card, he noticed the name of the 13th runner in a race – it was called 'Unlucky For Some' with odds at 13 to 1.

He surely had to bet on this horse. He'd keep up this theme and placed a £13 bet on the horse to win.

The horse ran, but came in 13th!

* * *

Small-minded

Eric was a mean, small-minded, unsavoury character, always was and always would be. His latest activity took him through some jungle. As he travelled along, he maliciously cut a rope bridge he'd crossed that hung over a fast-flowing river. He'd ruin or do anything disruptive. He laughed whenever he denied anyone the pleasure of doing what he enjoyed.

After a few hours he came to an area surrounded by sheer rock-face. He looked for a way to continue. A previous traveller had been helpful and left a sign, which read:

THE ONLY WAY BACK IS THE WAY YOU CAME.

* * *

Fund-raising

Thelma had agreed by telephone to help with local fund-raising for a new dialysis machine for the hospital. Brenda from the committee called on her to finalize the arrangements. "I think you are very brave," she exclaimed.

"Why, there's nothing to it," Thelma replied.

Brenda looked at her with admiration. "You are so calm about it."

"What's there to worry about, as I said, I do it often."

"To abseil down the Guildhall at your age takes a lot of courage, I certainly wouldn't have the nerve."

Thelma looked horrified.

"Abseil! I thought the girl on the phone said Boot-Sale."

* * *

Bankrupt

His forehead began to sweat. At one time he had wealth and owned lots of property. Now all had gone; he was bankrupt.

First of all the money ran out, then he started to sell the properties.

He had high hopes for better luck but things just got worse to the point of not being able to afford the rent on the last place he had.

Once or twice the threat of going to jail hung over him but he managed to avoid the indignity.

"Oh how I hate playing this stupid game of Monopoly!" he said, throwing the dice across the table.

* * *

3

Pearly Gates

Clive Barncroft stood at the Pearly Gates.

"I've been looking at your record on earth," began St Peter.

"Oh, I see." Clive looked surprised.

"I have noted that for the last thirty years you have been hunting with dogs."

"I can't deny that," retorted Clive.

"Have you heard of reincarnation?" asked St Peter.

"Yes, that's being reborn as someone else," replied Clive.

"Well this is how it works, you are only reincarnated once. I believe that you love the countryside, is that not so?"

"I certainly do," Clive said.

"That's good, because we are sending you back as a fox."

* * *

Fine at Forty

"You're forty years old today, whoever would believe that if you told them, I mean, just look at you!" She began brushing her hair.

"There isn't a grey hair to be found, and when you smile – sheer heaven. Your skin is so smooth, and you have kept your young and attractive slim figure. Your eyes are bright and teeth are white, what more could you ask for. You are in fact beautiful, any man would find it hard to resist your charm and modesty."

She stopped talking to her reflection in the dressing-table mirror and got dressed.

* * *

Gossip

People gossip in all walks of life. This little northern industrial town was no different. Houses joined onto one another with over the garden wall tittle-tattle. This pastime is of course not normally malicious, there are not many people who wouldn't have at one time indulged.

"The house at number 4 is a disgrace, Mrs Bradly's unattended pond water is stagnant," said one of the ladies to her neighbour.

Information was passed along the line of houses in the street. When the knowledge eventually reached number 104 it had changed to:

"It's a disgrace, Mrs Bradly's underage blonde daughter is pregnant."

* * *

The Fortune Teller

Gypsy Rose Lee began the fortune-telling of Mary Cummings. "You have a problem with one of your family," she declared.

"I have no family!" Mary answered.

"You will be going on a long journey," suggested the gypsy.

"Impossible, I run a nursing home and must always be on hand."

Everything the gypsy spoke of was disregarded by reasoning. The fortune teller brought the session to a close. "You will shortly be coming into a large sum of money… My fee is £10."

"You'll get nothing now, but I'll pay you £100 when I receive the large sum of money you've foreseen."

* * *

The Judge

The area filled quickly in anticipation of the summing-up and verdict.

All went quiet, you could have heard a pin drop.

The judge's mouth was dry. He'd been a little apprehensive of the outcome, given so many options to consider. Somehow he could not get rid of the lingering strange taste in the back of his throat.

Why was today any different than any other time he'd presided over the proceedings?

As he began to speak, he thought to himself: 'This is the last time I'll be judging the home-made jam making competition at the county fayre.'

* * *

Chemistry

He looked at the two test tubes in front of him.

"I believe I have the answer to everlasting life and to increase the size of living tissue," he murmured. But what effect would that have on the World, he considered. The food supply for a start, space, pensions, housing, traffic etc. etc. "No, no, no!" He went at once and poured the contents down the toilet.

"Put that chemistry set away, Tommy, you'll be late for school," his mother angrily called.

Later that month the headlines in the newspapers read:

'RATS TWICE THEIR SIZE FOUND IN SEWER.'

The mind boggles!

* * *

Granddad

"A story, Granddad, don't confuse us like last time."
  "I'll try," he beamed.

> *"It was a sunny day with heavy rain*
> *So I went to the airport to catch a train*
> *The boat was late I used the car*
> *I walked a long way for it wasn't far*
> *Rowing with ease as I swam the street*
> *My arms were aching, I rested my feet*
> *The wind was calm and blew so hard*
> *I ended up in my own backyard*
> *If I'd known of the stress and strain*
> *I'd have stayed at home and gone out again."*

They were not amused.

* * *

Kindly Soul

Lord Mitcham saw from his car window a man down on his luck. Mitcham was a kindly soul and requested his chauffeur to stop.

"Come home with me, my man, for a meal and a change of clothes."

He took the down-and-out into his kitchen. The door was ajar and the homeless man saw two men dressed worse than he was. Not knowing that they were two of the family going to a charity Tramps Ball, the tramp got up to leave.

"Where are you off to?" Lord Mitcham asked.

"I'm not stopping, I don't like the company you keep!"

* * *

The Smoker

Stella found her 13-year-old son smoking a cigarette.

"Where on earth did you get that from?"

"From a friend," her son replied sheepishly.

She sat down with him and explained the dangers of smoking. To emphasise the fact, she said, "Smoking stunts your growth."

At the weekend they boarded a bus to go into town. At one of the stops, two midgets from a nearby circus got on and sat opposite them.

"Coo, Mum, they must be smoking 60 a day," he shouted so all could hear.

His mother wished the earth would open up and swallow her.

* * *

Brave Lad

It was at the Bravery Awards ceremony. A young boy was called to the stage. The audience loudly applauded.

"You are an exceptionally brave lad," the presenter said with sincerity.

"Going into a burning building and saving a baby from certain death is one thing, but going back into that building three more times to see if anyone else were there is beyond belief, such heroism."

The boy looked embarrassed.

"I admit I saved the baby, but the reason I went back three more times was because my braces got caught on a knob on the banister in the hallway."

* * *

The Magician

The magician on board a cruise ship asked for a volunteer. Henry obliged.

The cabinet was shown to the audience to be empty. The back and sides were opened and walked through by his assistant.

Henry was placed inside. The doors were closed ready for the disappearing trick. At that precise moment the ship began to roll and sink. Henry got a blow to the head as the ship listed violently, knocking him unconscious.

When he came round, he found himself in the middle of the ocean.

"This is one hell of an illusion!" Henry muttered in amazement and admiration.

* * *

Endora

Endora the witch, with a wart on the end of her grotesque nose, sat in front of a large black cauldron consulting a book. The rest of the coven were out on their broomsticks, leafleting for the Liberal Demobats party.

In the pot went newt, toad, rat, the webs of ten large spiders, a handful this, a few drops of that, and so on. Every time she added something, she screamed; "Ah-ha-ha-ha-hah."

Two witches returned.

"What wicked potion are you concocting from that spell-book, to harm the Gories and Labourites," they screeched.

"This is a cookbook! That's soup for supper, you morons!"

* * *

The Waiter

A man went into a restaurant in Rome and sat at a table. The waiter came.

"Wada-you-a want-a?" he asked.

The man ordered a main meal and a cup of coffee.

The waiter returned and rudely slammed the plate of food down hard, causing some of the peas to roll across the table.

"Here-a you-are-a," the waiter said.

He did the same thing when he brought the coffee, spilling some of the liquid in the saucer. "You-a-want-a anything-a else-a?"

"What I would like is a little civility," the man replied.

"If-a eets not-a on-a the menu we don't-a serve eet."

* * *

Danger Flight

The day started calmly with full sunshine. Later on it became overcast, giving way to powerful gusty winds.

Flying now would be hazardous in both taking off and landing. Nevertheless, the flight had to be made before nightfall for her survival.

She took off precariously, feeling the strength of the wind on the wings; avoiding being blown off course.

In a longer time airborne than anticipated, the bluebottle had flown clear of the many spider webs that were spun ready to trap her. She landed safely on the warm and comforting compost heap, able to live and fly another day.

* * *

Some Dentists!

Two very good friends from boyhood decided to become dentists as their professions.

They both trained hard together and in the fullness of time passed with flying colours to become Dental Surgeons.

"Let's open a shared practice," suggested Ian.

"That's a very good idea, we've always been pals and we should work well together and make a fine living," replied Umberto.

"There's only one thing wrong with that, our names don't exactly give confidence to our prospective customers – now do they! Can't help the names we're christened with. Imagine seeing I. Pullum and U. Gummy on our appointment cards.

* * *

Forgetful – Never!

There was a knock on the door. Carole answered, it was her mother.

"Hello, Mum, what are you doing here today? You said you were coming on Wednesday."

"Did I?" her mother said, "never mind, on the way down I've bought you the bananas you wanted."

"No, Mum, I'm making an apple pie... I'll make us a cup of tea. When you get older, you have to write everything down in case you forget them."

"Oh, I know, the trouble is, I forget where I've left the bit of paper that I have written the things on."

* * *

Longer Short Stories…

The Chief Inspector

The Chief Inspector of police entered the room. His sergeant greeted him and stated: "Very unusual case this, sir, very unusual indeed. Never seen anything like it in all the years I've been on the force. He's been hanged, electrocuted, shot and stabbed."

Without saying a word, the Inspector removed his hat and coat and placed them on a chair. From the corner of his eye, he saw a bunch of grapes in a bowl in the middle of a coffee table. He strode over and helped himself to a handful.

"I wouldn't have touched these if he'd been poisoned," he said with a rueful smile, as he popped a few in his mouth.

The sergeant gave him a look of disapproval, but would not dare rebuke his senior.

The Inspector finished the grapes. "Right then, Sergeant, let's make a start. You've disturbed nothing I hope?"

"Certainly not," he answered curtly.

The Inspector looked meticulously around the room, making notes as he went. When he had completed his inspection, he said calmly, "Suicide."

"Suicide!" his sergeant gasped, looking at his superior in amazement.

"Oh yes, take note – he has no shoes on and his socks are wet. This is what happened: He placed the noose over his head and around the neck, then he kicked the chair away. His feet landed on the metal plate plugged in at the mains, which released an elasticised cord, which in turn pulled the trigger of the gun. The gun flew through the open window and tugged at a spring which released the dagger. If you look outside in the bushes you will find the gun."

"But why go to all that trouble to kill himself?" his sergeant inquired tactfully, so as not to upset his chief, in disbelief.

"Well now, that's for us to find out," the Inspector mused.

The curtain came down on Act 3 of the play.

*

Three days later the headline news on radio, television, and in the newspapers was that the actor who played the victim in the stage play *Murder Times Four* had been found drowned.

* * *

New Girlfriend

To make a good impression on his new girlfriend, he told her he was an excellent cook. If he'd told the truth, he would have said that he could hardly boil an egg let alone prepare a full meal properly.

He invited her one evening to his flat for dinner, but before she was due to arrive he would have a set meal for two, delivered earlier from a first-class restaurant, which would be placed in his kitchen. All he had to do was to heat it up. He could manage that. He'd bought plenty of cheap takeaways in his time.

This would not be a cheap takeaway. The chef at the restaurant where he intended to buy, had first-class culinary certificates to his name, and was well-known for his cuisine.

Earlier in the week he bought himself a white apron, to use on the evening of his girl friend's arrival. He wanted to look the part.

The time had come; it was seven o'clock. He sat and waited patiently, dressed to impress.

The doorbell rang, she was on time. He looked around to make sure all was in order. He let her in and warmly gave her a kiss.

"Something smells good," she said, her mouth watering to the aroma that wafted from the kitchen.

"The best is yet to come. I'll take my apron off after I dish up," he said with a cunning smile.

He came back into the room with the food and they sat down at a candlelit table with soft music playing in the background. You could not fault him on creating a perfect romantic atmosphere.

"How was the meal?" he asked, after they had eaten.

"Absolutely delicious," she remarked with satisfaction. She felt she'd found a treasure, she wouldn't be looking for another boyfriend in a hurry, that was for sure.

"Do you like to cook?" she asked. "Or do you find it a chore?"

"I love cooking," he instinctively lied. "You could say it's more like a hobby to me."

*

The following week she invited him to her house for a meal and to meet her parents. "Come nice and early," she said.

When he arrived she took him around the back of the house directly to the kitchen.

"I know I've got a bit of a cheek, and hope you don't mind," she said thoughtfully, "but I was so impressed with the food you cooked – and as you love cooking so much, and enjoying it as a hobby – I've got everything here you'll need to prepare an evening meal for us all. I told Mum and Dad how good you are and they can't wait to taste it!"

* * *

Retirement

Jenkins was about to retire after many years' loyal service to his company. He worked for them man and boy, and really put his heart and soul into his employment. The firm reluctantly had to part company with him and were rather sad to lose such a devoted employee. It would be hard to find a replacement. He was always on time.

On his last day at the office they gave him a farewell party to show their appreciation. The firm spared no expense to give him a good send-off. Tables and some of the desks were covered with trays of the best buffet cuisine, plus a selection of fine red and white wines.

They asked him to say a few words.

He looked around the room at their keen and friendly faces.

"I've always been dogged by time," he said. "Get up on time, catch the train on time, get to the office on time. Lunch time, back on time. Time, time, time, even the word annoys me. When I was a young boy, my mother used to regularly say: 'night time, come on, bedtime.' Even in bad weather at school and you did not want to go into the playground, the teacher would say 'come on, don't stay in the classroom, go outside it's playtime.' Before my promotion from the shop floor to office responsibilities, I've worked time and a quarter, time and a half, double time, short time. I read the *Times* newspaper on the train to work, I take the *Sunday Times* at home, but no more. I will retire and forget all about time."

"Not quite, Jenkins," the Managing Director said. "I... er... have to present you with er... we are giving you a chiming clock."

* * *

Lotto

Sam Atkinson had never been a gambling man. Never once bet on horses, dogs, football pools, scratch cards, slot machines or any other form of game of chance. Perhaps his strict upbringing by his parents had something to do with it. They both attended church regularly. His mother and father were not wealthy but of hard manual working class. They only had a minimal, but to them an adequate, amount of money coming in each week. Speculation and quick-rich schemes were frowned upon as being immoral. He was taught at an early age that only hard work and dedication would bring true rewards.

Sam was well liked by his neighbours and friends, an easy-going person who always paid any money owning on household bills etcetera, on time. He would never, under any circumstances, have or use a credit card, and never got himself in debt beyond his means. Credit card companies with offers to him to have one were continually coming through his door, ending up in the waste bin. There were many things he would have wished to have bought – a car especially, but the running costs were high and getting into that situation was taboo by his standards. He was however tempted at long last to have a small wager on the Lotto. Everyone else appeared to be doing it, so why not him he reasoned. And, after all, it would only be a small amount that he would wager; and the money the National Lottery collected went, by all accounts, to good causes.

Some of his friends had chosen birthday dates for the six numbers required, but birthday dates only go up to 31. Others had used door numbers of friends and family, but again they were also limited in choice as they could only go up to 49, and of course door numbers go on well above 49.

"How can I select my six numbers?" he pondered uneasily. He was told by one of his friends that he could select a Lucky Dip for the six numbers but thought that not to his liking.

He was due to go into town to pay a few bills, get monthly statements from his bank and do some shopping, and hoped to be inspired along the way. With that in mind he placed a small notebook and pen in his inside pocket. There were many shops in the High Street that sold lottery tickets, he'd seen the signs often enough. He freshened himself up and set off. It had rained heavily during the night and early morning but was now fine. At the bus stop, the first bus he saw coming along at a distance was the number 27 to Marshampton.

"Ah, that's the first number," he said to himself, and quickly wrote it down.

The bus was travelling quite fast and did not stop. It went through a deep puddle of dirty rainwater close to the pavement, drenching Sam from head to foot. He gave up the idea of catching a bus and decided to walk to the railway station to dry off a bit and catch a train instead. A little way down the road, children were playing and disturbed some pigeons that were feeding on some bread that had been thrown down for them. Five of the pigeons were flying and fluttering together.

"My next number has got to be 5," he assured himself, and penned it in.

As the birds flew over him, pigeon mess dropped and landed on his clothing. He wiped it off as best he could with a paper tissue, cursing under his breath.

Sam continued on his way reaching the station. At the pay window he bought a return ticket. Inside the station the number 40 train waited at the platform.

"The third one must be 40," he said, and down it went on the page of his notebook. As he got into the compartment of the train, he caught his sleeve on something jagged and ripped it. "Damn and blast," he said angrily. "I should have stayed in bed."

The journey was quite a short one, only one station away. Off the train at his destination and heading towards the town centre, two drunks were singing merrily coming from the opposite direction. He took out his pen and added to his list number 2.

He tried not to get too close to them but as he passed the drunks, one of them was shaking an opened can of beer; some of the contents squirted over him.

"Have a drink – have in drink – have a drink on me. Everybody have a drink on me, hey, hey, have a little drink on me," the drunks were singing.

"I'm beginning to feel and look a right old tramp," Sam thought, despondently. He pressed on in disgust not saying a word.

He arrived in the town square. The clock struck one.

"That's the fifth wanted – number 1," he murmured softly, and added it to the other numbers. Moving on and looking up at the clock, he trod in some dog's muck that lay in a heap on the ground.

"Not my day," he whispered, shaking his head and scraping his shoe on the ground, trying to dispose of most of it.

"Now let's see, I have 27 - 5 - 40 - 2 - 1, what shall I do to get the last number I want... I know, I'll count the steps on the way down from the town-hall after I have finished my business. But first and most important, what with the drenching I got from the bus, the pigeons' droppings, the beer squirted over me, my torn sleeve and the dogs' muck I trod in; a gents toilet in a large store or supermarket is a must, where they have liquid soap over the washbasins with hot and cold running water to sponge and clean myself up a bit."

It wasn't long before he came across, 'Best of Buys' Supermarket. Feeling much better for sprucing himself up in the gents wash room, he felt no longer like a down-and-out. Sam left the supermarket with renewed enthusiasm and wandered around, did some shopping, paid his bills, and got his monthly statements on his current and savings accounts. Much was on offer in the shop windows to tempt him; he overcame the urge, as he always did, not to buy any of them. He only bought the items that he'd set out to buy. He reached the town-hall with plenty of time to spare before his return journey home. When he had got his last number he wanted, he would purchase his lottery ticket on his way back to the station. Reaching the town-hall steps he began to descend slowly. He started the count diligently and reached step eight. Unfortunately for him, because he was not concentrating exactly where he was stepping, he misjudged the edge of the step, slipped and fell awkwardly to the bottom, badly bruised and breaking his right leg. The contents in his shopping bags tumbling out in all directions.

Passers-by stopped when they had seen what had happened and came to his aid. One called an ambulance because Sam could not stand up and was in a lot of pain. Another one kindly picked up his shopping items and returned them to the bags.

The ambulance was at the scene within about eight minutes. Sam was put on a stretcher and rushed to the Accident and Emergency Department at a nearby hospital. The X-ray showed a nasty break. He was operated on and his leg put in plaster.

Some hours later the doctor said, "You are very lucky, Mr Atkinson."

"Lucky! How on earth do you make that out?" Sam asked in astonishment and disbelief.

"Well, it's like this," the doctor replied, "with the ever increasing demand on the National Health Service and shortage of beds, there is an exceptionally long waiting list to get into this hospital, you could say it's more like a lottery."

After the doctor had gone, Sam felt let down, as he didn't get to count the last step at the Guildhall, to complete his six numbers; as he'd slipped on step 8. Could that have been an omen? If so, the six numbers would be: 27 - 5 - 40 - 2 - 1 – 8.

As at that moment in time, lying in a hospital bed, badly bruised and with a broken leg, those numbers weren't very lucky for Sam.

Could they be any luckier for you?

* * *

The Last Bus

He had missed the last bus. It didn't seem to matter, there just had to be a telephone box along the way to phone for a taxi. It was several miles out of town and he was none too pleased with himself for being so stupid as not to keep an eye on his watch; nevertheless he took such drawbacks all in his stride. One good thing in his favour was that the night sky was free from cloud and no immediate threat of rain. In fact, it was pleasant enough in the night air with only a gentle breeze blowing in his face.

After walking for approximately ten to fifteen minutes, he came across a call-box. "Ah, good, just the job," he happily muttered softly to himself. Fumbling in his pockets for small change, he opened the door and went inside. To his horror he found the phone had been vandalized, the lead torn from its socket. What if someone had been knocked down in a road accident and needed an ambulance urgently?

"Stupid, inconsiderate, mindless fools, all of them," he said out loud. It depressed him to read in the newspapers and to hear on television and the radio, of so many unpleasant news items of late. The mind could hardly take in some of the high positions that a number of the offenders held: Policemen, Doctors, Judges, Priests etcetera. Their crimes were horrendous, especially when it involved young children. They were only in a minority, unfortunately that was all it took to give their professions a bad name. If you can't trust these people, who the hell can you trust. It sickened him to think about it. Yes, so, so depressing. Very little good news was reported it seemed, good news hardly made sensational headlines for the tabloids.

It was a blessing, he thought, that a lot of people possess mobile phones these days, and could be used in an emergency, but as yet he wasn't one of them. After finding this damage to a public phone box, he might well think of getting one. But there again, people were being robbed of them, even in broad daylight, and not only children were victims. He knew of a friend who was mugged at knifepoint during the day by four youths, who took his money and his mobile phone. The ordeal was still giving him nightmares and he was now very nervous when going out on his own.

He shook off his melancholy mood and set off again hurriedly, with the prospect of walking all the way home. The moonlight was bright and he could see plainly quite a good way in front of him.

Only a few moments it seemed had passed after leaving the call-box, when a red-coloured Bentley car pulled up alongside him and stopped.

"Want a lift?"

He looked at the face of the person who had spoken, to find it was that of a young woman. Her voice was pleasant and from what he could see of her, very attractive.

He stood there motionless for a while, considering the offer. It was most tempting, but he said: "If you had been a man, I would have probably said, yes please. I thank you very much for the offer, but don't you realise how dangerous it can be to invite a complete stranger into your car. After all, you don't know me from Adam. You leave yourself vulnerable and open to robbery, rape and even being murdered. Terrible things are happening all the time," he said forcefully.

She did not comment immediately and appeared unconcerned. She smiled and then said, "I don't see the problem – men and women are more on equal terms these days, women are no longer looked upon as the weaker sex. Look at the jobs women do today; driving lorries and coaches, they even fly planes and are first class pilots."

She paused and then said, "You are going in my direction and you could give me a few directions to where I am headed when we get farther down the road."

He could hardly believe how naïve and trusting some people can be.

"Good God, don't you read the papers. Please, I beg of you," he went on, "lock your doors, wind up the windows and go wherever you're going. This has nothing at all to do with equality, or of women being the underdogs, it's a question of personal safety. Never give anyone a lift when you are on your own, especially at this time of night and out here in the countryside. It shouldn't be that way, but it is. I don't know what the world's coming to."

"I can look after myself, thank you," she remarked with just a little agitation. "You strike me as being a very genuine, concerned and considerate man, and would do no harm to anyone – hop in, it's OK. It would be nice to have your company."

Again he took his time to considerer her invitation. "It's very nice of you but no, please get on your way and take my advice. There are a lot of weirdoes about, believe you me. I'm not one of them, but you're not to know that, are you?"

She was running out of patience because of his stubbornness. "So then, that's your decision. Alright, if that's what you want and I can't persuade you otherwise, so be it," she said indifferently.

Revving the engine loudly she drove on.

He watched, deep in thought, as the rear lights of the car disappeared in the distance. She was a young woman that would not succumb to manipulation. A woman no doubt with strong willpower and assertiveness and perhaps a little arrogant, but definitely incapable of recognising a dangerous situation, he was sure. He hoped she would take his advice and not hear in the future that she had come to any harm.

Of what he saw in the moonlight, she was not short of money. The car she drove must have cost quite a lot of cash when it was brand new. He put these worrying thoughts to the back of his mind and continued on his way.

Over the police radio came an announcement to all mobile units:

"Young female with blonde hair, cut short, five feet seven tall; escaped from the mental wing of Romley prison. A clothing shop a mile away from Romley had been broken into and her prison clothing had been found. If the woman in this bulletin is seen, report to headquarters immediately. Proceed with extreme caution as she is in possession of a large kitchen knife. A nurse and warder were seriously injured when she made her flight for freedom. She is known as the Black Widow by the authorities because she was responsible for deaths of at least eight men. She is believed to be driving a stolen red Bentley car."

* * *

The Doorbell

The door bell rang several times. Bob woke up, switched the bedside table-lamp on, rubbed his eyes and looked at the clock. It was half past one in the morning. He put on his dressing gown and slippers and went downstairs to the front door. He opened it. A young man stood there. "I'm selling Double Glazing," he said with a broad smile, sticking his foot in the door.

"Double Glazing! Double Glazing! At half past one in the morning, you must be off your rocker – nutty as a fruit cake – mad as a hatter!"

"I've got a tape measure, I can quickly measure up, I won't take long, be gone in a jiffy. I can give you a discount on the price that you won't get from other firms."

"You're as barmy as they come, it's almost pitch black out there," said Bob.

"If you put all the lights on in the house, it would be a great help. A ladder and a pair of steps would be useful too," the young man said, still smiling.

"You must take me for a complete fool, you've got to be joking, waking me up from a sound sleep at this time of the morning. Never in all my life have I witnessed such idiotic audacity. The sheer cheek you have, makes my blood boil. It's bad enough being disturbed time after time and having to put up with unwanted calls on the telephone. I've a good mind to report you to your company," grunted Bob.

"No don't do that. This is my first job and I've only worked for them for three months," pleaded the young man.

Bob yawned and with a sigh said: "Let's both stop this larking around, son. It's very late and I'm dead tired. We all need some sleep. Be quiet and don't wake your mother on the way up. What did you do – forget your door key again, you idiot?"

* * *

29

Millionaire

A very brief description of Peter Marsdon would be to say that he is unmarried, unattached and a multimillionaire. He'd come to the stage in his life when he felt that he should meet the right girl and settle down. His concern was that he might be taken in by a gold-digger, one who would marry him not because she loved him but for his vast sum of money. It terrified him thinking of how long a marriage like that would last, and at what cost to his sanity.

He confided in a friend who was also the Sales Director of a company he held a large number of shares in. They'd known one another for many years.

Peter asked, "What would you do, Ted, if you were me? now that you know what's been eating away at me. You're a wise old bird – I should nickname you the owl."

Ted was flattered and gave a lot of thought to the question before answering. Then it dawned on him.

"If you'd be interested, old son, we will require someone to fill in for a while as a sales representative." He waited for a reaction from Peter, but it didn't come. As there was no immediate objection, he carried on, "You wouldn't be treading on anyone's toes – at least, not in the short term. You see, there are holidays coming up and one of our reps is recovering from a motoring accident. You wouldn't be putting anyone out of a job. You could, if it appeals to you, come and voluntarily work for say, three or four weeks or so for the company. You don't need the money, I'm well aware of that. It may be an opportunity to see how the other half lives. It's quite in order to donate any money we pay you to a charity of your own choosing. Identify yourself by some other name on the calls you make if you wish."

Ted paused and grinned. "You won't find many gold-diggers after a rep's salary," he advised jokingly.

To Ted's surprise, Peter accepted his friend's offer and after being given some simple basic training, started to cover areas where most of the work was to take repeat orders and introduce new product lines to those outlets. Not an over-demanding pressure on him. He had no sales targets to meet as other permanent reps were required to do so in that line of business.

A couple of weeks passed and he fell into the mundane job with pleasure, an entirely different way of life, giving him the experience of seeing how others earned their living. He met, spoke and laughed with different types of characters but as yet had not come across anyone likely be, Miss Right.

It must have been roughly three weeks since he'd started his new-found temporary occupation, when on calling on one of the regulars, he noticed a new young female face.

"You're new here, aren't you?" he inquired gingerly.

"Yes I am... I'm Julie Saunders."

"I thought I hadn't seen you before, hello... I'm John Harrison," he said untruthfully. He smiled at her and went on to say, "hope all goes well for you, see you later."

"Thank you." She smiled back at him.

John, as he was now, finished his business and left.

Back in Ted's office, Ted said, "How's it going, old son, you amaze me by sticking it out. I had my doubts on whether you would last a week. Some of our customers can be rather tricky to deal with. You've proven me wrong. Have you met your Miss Right yet, among the not-so-rich and fameless?"

"I'm not sure, but yes there is someone I could be interested in. I've met a charming young lady and she is quite pretty. Just have to see how it works out. She may be spoken for."

Each time he called at Julie's work place, he managed to see her. Their conversations became longer. They found they had a lot in common. He felt more and more attracted to her. On one occasion he took the bull by the horns and asked simply; "Are you going out with anyone?"

"No," she said, "there's no one, no one at all."

"I wonder then, would you care to go out with me one evening. We could have a meal or take in a show or something; whatever you would like to do."

After a moment's hesitation she replied, "I would like that very much."

The time passed by and they saw quite a lot of one another. They enjoyed each other's company and it was turning slowly into a romance.

At Ted's office one day, Ted announced: "The sales force is almost back to full strength, Peter. On the 5th of next month you will have to terminate your short career with us. I hope you have gained from the time you've spent on the road. I must say you've done a damned good job, old son."

Peter said, "Thank you, Ted, I wouldn't have missed it for the world. It's been a wonderful time."

That evening he had to meet Julie. It was time to put his cards on the table. It was not because his time was running out with the masquerade job. He had already made up his mind long before the meeting with Ted.

"Hello, darling," he said as Julie came towards him.

She got in his car and gave him a kiss.

Peter said lovingly, "I'm deeply in love with you and would very much like you to marry me... that's if you'll have me."

Julie looked at him with tenderness in her eyes. "I love you too – of course I'll marry you, but you know very little about me. Nothing would suit me better than to be your wife. When would you like us to get married?"

"The sooner the better as far as I'm concerned. It's for you to choose, that's always the woman's privilege I believe, to name the exact day. But before you give me an answer, I have a confession to make and I hope after you've heard me out, you won't change you mind. You don't know that much about the real me."

She looked at him puzzled. "Go on," she said, really mystified at what he was about to come out with.

"My name is not John Harrison for a start, it's Peter Marsdon, I—"

She interrupted him. "Why for heaven's sake! Are you in trouble with the police?"

"No, no, nothing like that!" he said, and went on to give her a full explanation of his deception. After he got it off his chest, he waited for her response.

She burst into laughter. "You will never believe what I am about to tell you now. I don't work for the company you call at – my family owns it. My real name is Ann Somers."

It was his turn to be flabbergasted. "You must be the daughter of Michael Somers, the retail tycoon who has a chain of businesses all over the country and abroad."

She chose her words carefully. "I have been dated in the past by men who, after a short spell, have tried to obtain money from me for some hare-brained schemes and others who have been found out to be playboys; looking for someone to latch on to for the rest of their lives, looking for easy street. I also didn't want someone marrying me for my money, only for love. No, with us it's different. I love you and still want to marry you more than ever. It's going to be difficult for both of us to get used to calling each other by our real names. What a fairytale it's turned out to be, I could have chosen any of the other stores to work at in different locations, and we may never have met. It was a chance in a million."

"Two with millions!" he exclaimed, "and thank goodness, no gold diggers in sight."

* * *

33

Two Homes

Harry Smith, legally married, lives with his wife and two children in Portsmouth.

The house they live in was left to him by his grandmother in her will, which is situated in the district of Southsea. The seafront nearby has its attractions and bracing sea air. Only a short bus ride away one can reach the Portsmouth dockyard with its long naval history, where here lies Lord Nelson's flagship *HMS Victory*. As do the 19th-century *HMS Warrior* and the *Mary Rose* from Henry VIII's navy.

The selfsame man, Harry Smith, is bigamously married to a woman with one child in Southampton. At the Southampton address he is known as Harry Jones.

The house in Southampton is not as grand as the house in Southsea, not by choice but driven by what he could afford at the time. However it was spacious enough to have a small front garden.

How he got himself in this predicament of two marriages he would find it hard to explain. When he first married, he never for one moment believed he had it in his make-up to be wickedly deceitful. In contrast to his vows in church, that's exactly what he'd done. Harry never intended for such a situation to find himself in; it just happened. That was his reasoning, not his fault. A chance meeting with the other woman changed his uncomplicated life and led to an affair. He told her he was single and unattached. She told him she loved him and wanted to get married. He should have wisely told her the truth and left her then and there, but could not find it in his heart to walk away and leave her in tears. Later on in their relationship, she told him she was pregnant with his child, he then felt he should do the right thing and stand by her, and so came the bigamous marriage.

From there on the two homes became a way of life. He could not bring himself to come out with the reality to either of the two women. He dearly loved them both and that was how it was. He wouldn't always be young and strong. Rarely did he dwell on the possibility of losing his job. Many people were being made redundant these days. What would happen in later life, he would face that when it came. It didn't bear thinking about. In addition he knew he was breaking the law and had no idea what that entailed if ever found out by the authorities – would it be a caution, fine or imprisonment? Added to that, what reaction could be expected from the two women in his life?

He is a good husband and family man at both households, he loved all of his three children. He works hard at each abode; helping out whenever he can; mowing the lawns and generally keeping the properties in a respectable condition.

He was able to alternate his time spent between dwellings. Both women accepted his absence when he was not with them as his profession is not a 9 till 5 job, working long hours and nights away from home on a regular basis. There were never any awkward question from either wife he had to answer.

How fortunate he felt to be in the best of health and full of energy. The big problem being the cost of running two homes. On his excellent salary he just about managed – with quite a lot of manipulation to the outgoings. It was beneficial that both his wives had part-time jobs bringing in some money.

At the Portsmouth address, he had always paid the electricity bills on time but had a poor record with the Gas Company.

It was the other way round in Southampton. His payments to the Gas Company were perfect – in difference to the Electricity Company which were very bad, who were fed up with sending final notices for payment to him on a regular basis.

Similar to juggling his visits to the two homes so did he juggle the payments of any bills that came in; his method being that one would be paid in full, while the other would be paid when the final demand came in. This gave him that little extra time he needed to keep the payments ticking over.

One day when he was at home in Portsmouth, a man called on him. The man spoke very politely and had the gift of the gab with enthusiasm. He was smartly dressed in a dark-grey suit, fashionable shirt, collar and tie.

"Good morning, Sir, I'm from your electricity suppliers," he beamed. "If you buy gas from us as well as your electricity we can save you money." The caller went into details of how the system worked and how the saving could apply to him.

Harry's face lit up. "Sounds good to me," he said, and signed up.

When the Electricity Company checked their own records, they found him to be a good payer and pleased to have him on their books for both supplies. The Gas Company were relieved to get rid of him.

A week later when he was at home in Southampton, a lady called on him. She looked very presentable, smartly dressed and also had been trained in the gift of the gab for door-to-door calling.

"Good evening, Sir, I'm from your gas suppliers. If you care to take both your gas and electricity from us, you can save yourself a lot of money." She explained in fine detail how this could be done.

"That's excellent, yes I'll do that." He signed up on the spot.

The Gas Company looked through the time he had been with them to find he had always paid promptly. They accepted him for both gas and electricity supplies.

The Electricity Company were glad to see the back of him.

The Gas Company's happy. The Electricity Company's happy, and Harry is happy.

Now there is something fundamentally wrong here somehow. There's that old saying: *'Two Wrongs don't make a Right.'* In this case they did – well at least for the time being.

Life's complicated enough. Not many would swap with Harry … would you?

* * *

The Thief

Hermann, given any opportunity, would thieve. If you stood still long enough in one place, he would take the laces from your boots. He was a really nasty piece of work He had no sense of right and wrong or the feelings of those he robbed; no conscience whatsoever. Nothing he ever did kept him awake at night. Burglary and muggings were no stranger to him. He wanted the good life but had no intention of working for it. Others had to earn money, and he'd take it from them given the chance.

One overcast afternoon he saw and followed a little old lady down a quiet alley. He fixed his eyes on the bag she had slung over her shoulder. He quickened his pace and caught up with her. He checked to see no one was near enough to come to her assistance. In a split second he wrenched the bag violently from her and ran off.

He was panting a little as he let himself into his ground-floor flat. Once inside he opened the bag and attempted to shake the contents onto the table. To his surprise, only one object fell from the bag. He put his hand in the bag and rummaged around, hoping to find a compartment with something in it of value. His face twisted with disappointment, no banknotes, no coins, no credit cards, no savings book, nothing at all.

He picked up the one object that lay there, it was a small bronze medallion. He looked closer at it, hoping it was gold. Unfamiliar symbols were inscribed on it. He had no idea what they were or meant. With disgust he returned the medallion to the bag and threw it in the cupboard maliciously.

From that moment onwards events did not go in his favour. Nothing life-threatening, but whatever he did turned sour. When he shaved, occasionally he would nick his face with the razor blade, a thing he'd never done before with a safety razor. A bet he'd placed on a horse at the bookies, won, the ticket was lost. He looked everywhere for it without success. Just after breaking his watch, he was caught by a detector van for not having a television licence and made to buy one, plus an imposed heavy fine. To rub salt in the wounds, after grudgingly paying for the licence, his television caught fire and was useless.

Of course the television set was one he had stolen as well as the watch he had broken. In an attempted burglary to replace them, he was nearly caught red-handed in the process. He hurt himself severely by twisting his ankle, jumping from a window in his panic to escape from the house. He'd watched the house for some time at length, observing that the occupants were always out between certain times. The day he had a go at his burglary, the man of the house returned unexpectedly.

Any endeavour at skulduggery by him failed miserably. Money wasn't coming his way and he needed money fast, His landlord demanded the rent that had not been paid for some considerable time, more than likely he would be given notice to quit at any time. The thought of getting a job terrified him. Frantically he tried another mugging. On this occasion an elderly man was approached just as it was getting dark in the evening. Hermann threatened his victim with a knife menacingly, demanding money. The knife slipped from his hand, falling point down slicing through his right leather shoe, the tip of the blade piercing his big toe. Not only that, the old gent angrily hit him with his walking stick as he hobbled away as fast as he could manage. Absolutely nothing was going as he intended.

Late morning one day, fate guided him to the park. The weather was fine with little or no breeze. The sun was warm and people came into the park to enjoy it.

Sat on a bench feeding the birds, was the old lady he'd snatched the bag from. He walked slowly over and sat beside her. She stared at him.

"You know who I am, by the look of that stare, I can tell," he declared quietly.

"Oh yes, I know exactly who you are, I recognise you alright," she replied calmly.

"Look, I mean you no harm. I've got a conscience," he lied. "I want to return that bag I stole from you. Wait here, I'll go and fetch it."

"That won't do you any good. You've had bad luck ever since you stole it from me. That's why you want to give it back, you wouldn't know a conscience if it hit you in the face," she said with great satisfaction in her voice.

"Yeah, yeah, OK alright," he said reluctantly and with irritation. "But how on earth do you know that?"

She looked him straight in the eyes, her tone of voice sounded sincere. "When young people look at the old, they only see what they are now. They never take into consideration that old people were once young, fit and active like themselves. If only we knew what lives the old have lived. I was speaking to an old fellow a short while ago who could hardly hold his walking-stick, yet in his younger days was a fighter pilot in the RAF. You look at me now and see perhaps, a frail sweet old lady. Let me tell you this, when I was young I was no saint. I lived life to the full. One of my specialities was shoplifting. One day I stole a handbag, similar in a way to the manner you stole mine, inside was that medallion. My life changed badly from that day on. It took me some time before I realised it had something to do with that medallion. I tried to get shot of it. At first I gave it away, put it in a charity bag; it came back. I threw it in the sea, I even tried to burn it in a workman's brazier on a building site, to melt the damned thing down. It was back indoors again when I got home, it was frightening, I was at my wits' end to know what to do next, I was even thinking of taking my own life. With my luck at the time, it wouldn't have worked. If I had put my head in the gas oven, no gas would have come through the pipes."

She stopped talking briefly and looked across at the ducks on the pond, then continued with her story. "I don't know why, I suddenly realised that the only way of getting rid of it was the way I got it; it had to be stolen from me. I walked in crowded market places, shopping precincts, down quiet streets, but nobody took it until you came along. My life and luck changed immediately, I bought a scratch card and won £50. The problem is yours now. You will feel foolish of course if you do what I did. You don't see many men carrying a handbag. You'll have to think of another way won't you. Remember the next time you come across a defenceless old lady with a handbag, you might think twice before relieving her of it."

When she had finally finished speaking, his eyes wandered unintentionally for a few minutes to other parts of the park, deep in contemplation of all she had admitted. His brain was in complete turmoil. He had many questions on his mind to ask. He turned eagerly to face her but she had gone.

* * *

Ginger Cake

I had it in my mind that there is a difference between envy and jealousy. To me envy seemed to say: 'I would really love to have that, but no animosity to those that have.' Jealousy on the other hand I believed was something comparable to; 'If I can't have it, you shouldn't have it, and given the chance I'd take it from you.'

Looking through the dictionary, the meaning appears to be very much the same for both envy and jealousy. I would have put Adam Wallington in the jealous category had I been correct in my definition. He is married to Janet – they have no children. An upsetting time for Adam began when out shopping one day his wife met up with an old school friend, Margaret, she had not seen for many years. Janet invited her back home for a cup of tea and a chat about old times. Margaret was introduced to Adam. It did not take Adam long to take a dislike to her. She was smartly dressed and wearing enough jewellery to open a shop. She informed them that she was a widow now and left very well off financially. Her late husband being the Managing Director of a large company. She spoke of her new car, her fine house, the antique furniture, the enormous garden, holiday cruises to all parts of the world, and so on. Adam felt the pangs of resentment immediately.

Her visits to Janet became notably more frequent over the following weeks. Janet was invited to Margaret's house but Adam was not mentioned – he wouldn't have gone had he been included in the invitation. Adam was becoming increasingly resentful of the attention given by his wife to her friend and less to him. Dislike twisted into something more sinister. To Adam's further annoyance, Margaret began commenting: "Your lawn is in an appalling state, Adam, about time you cut it. This needs a lick of paint Adam, don't leave it much longer will you." The snipes at him kept coming. Her remarks were becoming increasingly personal each time she came to the house, had he shaved etc. His blood almost reached boiling point just to look at her. The sound of her voice grated on his nerves.

As it happened, Margaret was exceptionally fond of ginger cake, Adam and Janet could not stand the flavour of ginger. From time to time, Janet baked for her friend a ginger cake. She always took it away with her when she left their house. To his unease, it got to Adam that his wife would do almost anything for Margaret. The situation was becoming unbearable for him to live with.

Hate mixed with jealousy does not make a very attractive cocktail.

Adam had heard or read somewhere that apple pips contain a very minute amount of cyanide. Chewing and swallowing one or two pips would do no harm. Saving them up until you accumulated a jam jar full, and then chewing and eating them all at once, would make you seriously ill or probably kill you.

The months went by, Adam bided his time saving apple pips. When he had saved enough, he ground them down to a coarse powder, put them in an envelope and tucked it away in his inside pocket, waiting for his opportunity.

One particular morning, Adam came down to breakfast to find his wife making a ginger cake. He went to the sink and washed his hands. He made an excuse: "Is that someone tapping on the front door?" he ventured.

"I didn't hear anything," Janet replied.

"Go and see please, would you, I've got wet hands."

When she had gone, he dipped his finger into the bowl and tasted the contents. Adam screwed up his face in displeasure. Yes, most certainly ginger, he confirmed.

Without giving it a second thought, he then took the ground-up apple pips, shook them into the cake mixture and gave it a good stir.

Janet returned. "There was no one there!" she exclaimed, most annoyed.

"I must be hearing things, sorry," he said, apologetically. After breakfast he left the house and went to work.

When he returned home that evening, he asked casually, "Has your friend been round today? Give her the cake you were making this morning?"

"That wasn't for her, I had to make a cake for the Church fête," she told him.

He couldn't believe his ears.

"You don't usually make cakes for anyone else," he said, stunned.

"I was talked into it by someone from the church committee," Janet replied. "The money they make is going to a good cause I was told, so I didn't mind."

His face drained. "Where is this fête to be held and what time does it start? Are you going?" he asked indifferently but inwardly extremely concerned.

"At the church hall of course. Tomorrow at ten o'clock – and no I won't be there – I'm spending the day with Margaret."

Margaret! Margaret! Margaret! He could have strangled the woman.

The next morning Adam didn't go to work. He headed directly to the church hall. He arrived very early so as to be the first one there. He was lucky that no one pushed in front of him. The lady on the stall had Madeira, Coconut, Chocolate, Lemon, sponges and fairy cakes. There was only one Ginger cake. It looked like the one Janet usually baked. Adam paid for it, and went back to his car Now what should I do with it, he pondered. I can't feed the birds or the ducks on the pond. I daren't leave it anywhere. I can't bury it in the woods. Someone may think I'm burying a body. No such luck, if it had been Margaret, he'd gladly have taken the chance. If she had died of poisoning from the cake, would the police have been able to trace the cake back to his wife? Someone would have seen Janet and Margaret together on many occasions. And what would Janet have thought when she heard of the death of her friend – the tampered cake being the cause – what would she have made of that? He hadn't thought about that at the time. He hoped now that it would have only made her extremely ill and kept her away from the house forever.

Adam drove to a public toilet, broke up the cake and flushed it down the pan.

So as not be out of the ordinary, he returned home that evening at around about the same time as usual – pleased as punch with himself for buying back the cake and disposing of it. It was a great weight off his mind but had cost him, at least the loss of a day's earnings.

After eating his evening meal he went to the waste bin to scrape the leavings from his plate. He opened the lid and saw a baked ginger cake there. He made his way hurriedly back to his wife.

"What's that cake doing in the waste bin?" he inquired sourly.

"Oh that. That's the first cake I made yesterday morning. I left it too long in the oven and ruined it. I couldn't give that one to the fête, so I had to bake another," she remarked, unconcerned.

* * *

At the Supermarket

Melanie parked her car in the supermarket car park, easily finding a specially allotted 'mother and child' parking space. She and her four-year-old daughter got out of the car and collected a shopping-trolley from the bay. She carried a shopping bag – with a few earlier purchases she had made from elsewhere – which she kept by her side. The Supermarket was quite crowded with last-minute shoppers and bargain hunters. The store had many 'money off' and 'buy one get one free' offers on this week.

They went through the entrance and began to go up and down the aisles mingling with the other large number of people shopping there, selecting goods she required as she went, putting them into the trolley, stopping occasionally to compare prices on some of the different brand named items.

Now and again the little girl would pick up, quite casually, something from the shelves and gently drop it into her mother's bag that she carried by the side of her. This took place four times and Melanie seemed unaware what her daughter was up to, her eyes firmly focussed elsewhere.

They finished their shopping and queued at the checkout counter until it was their turn to be attended to. The contents of her trolley were processed through the pricing machine with the familiar bleep as each item was passed through. She paid for the goods and bagged them up, then moved her trolley away from the checkout to a wall. After checking the receipt, she placed it in one of the supermarket's own plastic bags with the purchases she'd made.

As they got just outside the door, and heading back to their car, a security guard stopped them. The security guard made quite sure he could not be overheard.

"Excuse me, Madam, would you please accompany me to the Manager's office," he said, quietly and discreetly.

"What on earth for?" she demanded.

"The manager would like a quick word with you please, I'm sure we can soon clear this up, Madam, if you would please follow me."

He lifted all her bags out of the trolley and set off in the direction of the store manager. She had little choice now but to reluctantly follow him.

In the manager's office, she was greeted by a very polite and pleasant man.

"Sorry to put you to this inconvenience, Madam, but our security cameras show your little girl putting some things in your bag unknown to you."

"I can't believe it, surely not," she said solemnly.

"Kindly empty the carrier bag that you carried by your side in the store, and you will soon see what I mean," the manager said sympathetically.

Melanie picked up the bag and carefully shook the contents onto a table. Amongst the items that had not been paid for from the store were; a small tin of salmon, a tin of cod's roe, a small tin of corned beef and a tin of crab.

Her face reddened with embarrassment.

"What can I say, I apologise most humbly. This is awful."

The manager began to put her mind at ease. "This is of no concern to the police, please do not be alarmed. Normally they would be called when there is a deliberate shoplifting case to be prosecuted. Stores up and down the country lose thousands and thousands of pounds this way and it is the general public that have to pay for it in the end by these stores having to put up the prices of products to pay for the loss. The prices in this store as in many others would be a lot cheaper if only we could stamp it out completely. We are doing our utmost to try to achieve this, but it is a slow and long process. More and more up-to-date technology keeps coming to help us. Naturally this is expensive and adds to the cost of running a business. I'll say no more on the subject. In this instance, your little girl is too young to really understand what's going on. Being a child of such a young age, I would not attempt to question her or upset her in any way. This matter will be taken no further this time. These goods will be returned to the shelves. You will of course be expected to explain to your daughter when you get home the merits and pitfalls of the situation, try to make her fully understand that items must only go in the trolley. Explain all products have to be paid for. If you shop here in future with your little girl, please make sure this type of behaviour by her does not happen again."

"It won't, have no doubt about that," she assured him.

"Good, then let's forget all about it. You may leave now, and thank you for your cooperation."

Melanie gathered her bags together with the items she'd paid for.

"I would like to express my sincere thanks for the way you've handled this upsetting state of affairs. I must confess I was a little disturbed when stopped outside. I had no idea what this was all about until now."

The manager smiled. "I have very young children of my own and am able to see both sides of the coin. Also it is the policy of the company that all staff – including myself – are trained to the highest standard in dealing courteously and fairly with our customers. After all, you have to use your common sense in these situations. I hope the security guard was also as diplomatic when you were stopped."

"Yes he was, most considerate," Melanie replied.

"That pleases me immensely to hear our high standards are upheld," he retorted happily.

As they reached the door to leave, the manager opened his desk drawer and took from it a bar of chocolate. "Wait a moment, little one," he called.

The manager went over to the little girl and gave the chocolate bar to her.

"Oh, thank you very much," she said. Her face brightened.

"What's your name?" he asked.

"Lucy," she replied sweetly.

The manager could not resist saying, "When you come to the store next time, don't put anything from the shelves in your mummy's bag, will you."

She looked up at him straight-faced. "No I won't. If mummy tells me to do it again, I will say no," Lucy answered reassuringly.

* * *

The Pilkingtons

I went to the Police Station and reported that my wife had not been home for two nights. Most of her personal belongings had gone, along with all of her clothing. She left no note, a holdall and three large suitcases were missing. She obviously left in someone's car or by taxi. It seemed odd, I told the officer, that there was no explanation of why she'd gone.

The policeman I spoke to was very understanding. He asked the usual questions of how long we'd been married, was there another man? etc. He explained that they did not have the resources to help me as it appeared to be a personal matter, and that I should think about hiring a private investigator. As a matter of routine, he took down both our names: Mr James Pilkington and Mrs Mabel Pilkington along with our address. He was also insistent that I let him know when she was found and that no harm had come to her, since I'd made an official statement to him of a missing person. It might have been in his mind that I'd done away with her by the way he looked at me when I left the station.

After searching through the telephone directory, I contacted and hired a Mr Paul Bailey who had very little trouble in finding her. His services didn't come cheap. I went along again to the police station and informed them that she had been found by Mr Bailey. They were pleased that I let them know the outcome of my concern. She was staying with her aunt temporarily, I informed the police. I didn't give any reason why she went or whether she would be coming back. The private investigator wondered why I could not have done the searching myself and saved the expense of paying him, as finding her was quite simple. She told him she did not want a divorce but she would never return home; as us being together in the house, with no grown-up children, had become tiresome and unbearable, slowly driving her to despair. She wanted the house sold and the money to be split between us equally.

She informed Paul Bailey that she trusted her husband to honestly make all the necessary arrangements and send her a cheque with copies of all the transactions to her new temporary address. To cut a long story short, this was done. A letter confirming all the private investigator had passed on to me, by word of mouth, was received. I then legally could proceed. The property was put on the market and quickly sold. The house and grounds are large and fetched a good price. I bought an old farmhouse in France with the intention of doing it up.

To all intents and purposes, Mabel left her aunt after a few months and moved on to pastures new.

All was going well until the people who bought our house decided that they would like a sunken garden and a pond. They called in a landscape gardening firm who started almost immediately on the work. During the alterations, a body was found and the police were called. It turned out more to be an excavation than an alteration. The detective in charge was a big irritable man with a face as long as a boring speech. The first task of the CID was to trace the previous owners and continue the inquiries from there.

These pathologists nowadays are brilliant, they go thoroughly into the smallest detail. Forensic medicine and dental records etc. brought to the conclusion that the body found buried was that of James Pilkington.

James Pilkington! But how could that be! The police had seen and spoken to Mr Pilkington when he called at the police station about his wife. They saw him again when he reported that his wife had been found by the private investigator. That was long after the corpse that had been found had died, according to the autopsy report. Mr Bailey had acted for him in finding his wife.

The estate agent who sold the house had done business with him. He was the one who handed over the deeds of the property. The solicitors had his signature – or did they?

It did not take a lifetime for one of the investigation team to go into the background of the Pilkingtons. I thought I'd been so clever with my charade and all the trouble I went to, leaving a false trail. They found out that I was on the stage as a male impersonator many years ago before I married. Now I must pay the price of life imprisonment. If only the new owners had left the garden alone I would have got away with it...

A hand is shaking my shoulder.

"Wake up, I've brought you up a cup of tea," James is saying tenderly.

James Pilkington! James Pilkington! My mind is in turmoil. I wake up to his voice. I am in my own bed, in my own bedroom, in my own home. My husband is alive, not dead. I did none of this scheming. I can hardly believe it.

I look up at him from my pillow. He places the tea tray on the bedside cabinet.

"I've had the most frightening dream. To be truthful a terrible nightmare," I confess, nearly bursting out in tears. My heart is pounding twice as normal.

How stupid dreams are. I have never been on the stage in my life, let alone impersonate anyone. It felt so real and believable. If the dream had not been so awful and alarming, I would surely laugh at the whole idea. As it was so bad, I feel more of a wonderful relief than anything else.

He's looking at me solemnly.

"I've told you before, more than once, not to eat cheese or read those dreadful murder stories last thing at night before you go to bed, haven't I!" James emphasises sternly.

He bends over and kisses me tenderly on my forehead, I respond giving him a big hug. I feel that I never want to let him go.

"In future I will definitely take your advice, that's a promise!"

There is banging coming from our old-fashioned heavy brass knocker. James goes down to answer the door. He's been gone a good five minutes; I was thinking of getting up. Then he returns.

"Who was that?" I ask.

"Someone from some landscape company, trying to drum up some work. Wanting to know if we'd be interested in having a sunken garden and a pond."

* * *

Insurance Claim

Vincent Carmichael waited patiently to drive out of a side road into a main road. It was a bright afternoon, there wasn't a cloud in the sky, visibility couldn't be better. The driver of a car on the main road did not allow enough space as he turned sharply into the side road. He collided and cracked the glass on the headlight and caused other damage to the metalwork on the front of Vincent's car. After a few heated words, both drivers pulled over to one side of the road and exchanged details for insurance purposes. As no one was injured, the police were not called. The other driver's name given to Vincent in the exchange was Damon Ravenscroft, who admitted to him that he was at fault, obviously acknowledging reluctantly that his mind had been temporarily elsewhere and not concentrating enough on his turn.

To Vincent's unbelief, his insurance company wrote to him sometime later informing him that Mr Ravenscroft's account of the accident differed from the one submitted by him, and that it was Vincent who had driven into Damon Ravenscroft from the side road. This letter caused him overwhelming anger and frustration. It also gave him many a sleepless night.

Through no fault of his own it was likely, Vincent felt, that he would lose his no claims bonus and his insurance premium would rise quite steeply. His insurance company stressed that a witness or witnesses to the accident would be an ideal solution in proving who had given a true account on their insurance claims forms.

Vincent told his friend Ken Williams all that had happened with regard to his unexpected letter from the insurance company and of his grievance at being the innocent party. "The thing is, Ken, I've never once claimed since I started driving. And now it's come as a complete shock – being accused of something I never did. If it had been my fault, fair enough, I would have accepted it without any qualms."

His friend looked at him long and hard in disbelief.

"The toerag, what a lousy thing to do," Ken said. "Some people make me sick. Why don't you go round and knock his block off."

"That would make it even worse. I daren't get in touch with him. Who knows what would happen if I confronted him with his lies. He knows, as well as I do, that cars on the main road have the right of way under normal driving standards. He also knows I was stationary at the time and that he drove into me, not the other way round… the lying devil, it makes my blood boil every time I think of it. It was entirely his fault, but I have no way of proving it now. It's his word against mine."

"Wasn't there anyone who saw what happened?" asked Ken.

"I haven't a clue, it all happened so fast, I never gave it a thought that I would need one. After all, no one was hurt, and he seemed to be a genuine sort of a guy."

"What are you going to do about it, Vince?" his friend asked wearily.

"I am hoping someone will come forward. I'm going to advertise in the local paper and stick a card in the newsagents on the corner of Carter Road; asking if anyone saw the accident at four o'clock on Thursday the 21st of September at the junction in London Road and Carter Road. I'll give my phone number and my insurers' name and address, and hope for the best. What else can I do?"

"I can say I saw the whole thing, Vince," Ken said helpfully.

"No, that would be most unwise. You would get yourself into serious trouble. If it went to court, you would have to perjure yourself, and we are friends. That wouldn't wash for a start. They want an independent witness. They might ask if you know me, and you would have to lie again and say you don't know me."

"Who would have any knowledge that we are friends? I live some distance from you. Not as though we live in the same street or work together."

"You're a very good friend, Ken, It's illegal and you don't know what you'd be letting yourself in for. I'm most grateful for the thought, but no thank you."

A week passed by and nobody had phoned Vincent with regard to the accident. His hopes were sinking fast and it made him feel down in the dumps.

Ken met Vincent by chance one Saturday in the market place.

"Let's go for a coffee, Vince, I've got something to tell you," said Ken.

They found a quiet café and settled themselves at a table in a corner with their drinks.

"I know you said no, but I've written to your insurers, Vince. I told them I saw the whole thing. How a car on the main road swung round into the side road and collided with a stationary car. I said I saw the advert for a witness to come forward. That should get them off your back."

"Crikey! You shouldn't have done that, Ken, hopefully someone else may have written to my insurers, but I wouldn't take bets on it. You know these insurance companies, they are long-winded when it comes to paying out, but quick to remind you when your policy renewal date is due," he said despondently.

"So be it, it's done now. If someone else writes in, it's a bonus. I can't undo what I have done," said Ken with a martyred look.

And very long-winded the insurers were, it took weeks before Vincent heard from them. When it came he opened the letter anxiously; to his surprise, it was excellent news.

They concluded that in view of a witness statement being received by them and a copy forwarded to Mr Damon Ravenscroft's insurers, the outcome was that they have now accepted responsibly and had agreed to settle his claim in full.

The next time Vincent met Ken he told him what had happened.

"That's taken a lot off my mind, Vince. Justice has been done in the end. I would like to have been a fly on the wall when this Ravenscroft chap had to eat humble pie. I wonder what he said to his insurers when they proved he'd been economical with the truth? I'm pleased it's all over, I don't think I could do that again. It has played on my conscience a bit."

"And nor you should, Ken, thank God it didn't backfire on you – and me come to that."

"If there had have been a genuine witness, surely you could have sued him for defamation of character or something."

"As things stand at the moment, I'm more than happy to let sleeping dogs lie," emphasised Vincent.

A while later one evening, Ken was relaxing in his lounge watching television. He was about halfway through the programme and enjoying it. If he'd known of what was to come that evening he would have recorded it for another time.

The doorbell rang and disturbed his comfort. Ken answered the door grudgingly. Two well-dressed men stood there. One was on the stout side, the other was lean and with cold observant eyes. Ken looked at them in surprise. If they are selling something I'm liable to be most unpleasant, he thought to himself. He glanced at them keenly, waiting for the sales talk.

"Good evening, Sir," one of them said. "I'm DI Jones and this is Detective Sergeant Nickles." They produced and showed him their warrant cards.

Ken was even more surprised. Why were they calling on him, he wondered.

"Are you a Mr Ken Williams?"

"Yes, that's me," said Ken.

"Would you mind answering a few questions?" DI Jones inquired. "May we please come in?"

"Yes certainly, if I can. By all means, come on in."

They were shown into the living room and offered a seat. Ken went and turned the television off. They all sat down.

"Now how can I be of help?" asked Ken.

"You wrote to an insurance company about having seen a motor accident on the 21st September at four o'clock." DI Jones' tone was soothing yet blunt and to the point.

"Yes, I did. Surely that's not serious enough to be a police matter," Ken said, his heartbeat quickening. "I didn't see anyone get hurt."

"No, it's not actually to do with the accident itself. There was a robbery at a jeweller's in London Road at about 3.55 p.m. on the 21st of September. You were only a matter of minutes or so away in walking distance from the shop and we are keen to find anyone who witnessed the event take place." The detective paused for a moment, then said: "What happened was a man about your age, went into Marks the Jeweller's and asked to see a tray of gold rings. He didn't appear to be acting suspiciously but waited until the shop was empty of customers. He picked out the most expensive one from the tray. He then asked if he could try it on. The young lady assistant said 'yes'. He put it on his finger and ran out of the shop."

Sergeant Nickles took out a notepad and waited for his colleague to ask relevant questions.

Questions were asked of Ken of where he set out from, and where he was heading to that afternoon in question.

Which side of the road he was on, etcetera. Ken had to give a reasonable, but an untrue account of himself. When Ken had answered these questions, the detective said: "Now what I want to know is, when you passed the jeweller's, did you see anything that might help us? Anyone running out of the shop or rushing past you, where he may have gone – a waiting car, anything at all."

He took from his pocket a brown envelope that contained photos from the security camera at the jeweller's. "This is the man we would like to interview." The detective glanced at them as he passed them to Ken.

"Heavens above! It could be you. The likeness is incredible," the detective exclaimed.

"That's utterly absurd. I'd hardly rob a jeweller's and give my name as a witness to an accident being near the place I robbed… now would I?" Ken was forcing his brain to work harder. He could prove he was nowhere near London Road when the robbery took place, but he had borne false witness to an accident, to help a friend he knew was genuine in all he said and had done. There was no way now of going back on it.

The detective noticed that Ken was not wearing any rings on his fingers.

"Not as if it matters I'm sure, but you have no ring marks. I take it you don't wear them?"

"Never have, but I don't expect this chap stole the ring to wear, most probably needed money – perhaps for drugs," replied Ken, indulgently.

"Would you be prepared to come to the police station at a later date and take part in an identity parade?" the detective asked formally.

Ken thought, what sort of mess have I landed myself in. He squeezed out the words, "I'd be more than happy to do so. I'm positive that the shop staff will see that I am not the culprit. I never saw anything with regard to this robbery you are investigating. Sorry I cannot help you. No one acting suspiciously that I saw that afternoon."

The two detectives got up from their seats. They both stared at him, making him feel uncomfortable. "If you are sure you cannot help us any further with our inquiries, then that will be all for now, Mr Williams. We may possibly like to see you again. We will be in touch," DI Jones said, looking again at him with his cold observant eyes. They both left the house.

Ken returned to his seat in the lounge in a remorseful mood. He couldn't settle. He got up and filled a kettle for a cup of tea. Another interruption, the letterbox flat snapped, something had been pushed through it. He went to the door and picked a pamphlet up from the doormat. It was a religious pamphlet. He looked at it and read:

> *'The Lord works in mysterious ways.*
> *Be sure your sins will find you out.'*

He went to the kitchen and made his tea, then went to the front door again and opened it. He looked out and up and down the street. An elderly lady and a young girl were still putting pamphlets through the letterboxes on the other side of the street. He looked up at the clear night sky. The stars were twinkling. With raised head he uttered under his breath: "I've got the message."

Snake Ring

Paul Davidson arrived outside the two large wrought iron gates of 'Chorley House'. The young fair-haired man got out of his car, and straightened his tie. There was also a small pedestrian gate to the left of the main gates. His appointment was for seven o'clock – it was now a quarter to seven – he had fifteen minutes to spare. The journey time had been judged well.

He stretched his legs, got back into his car and slowly drove towards the house. On either side of the driveway were borders, growing a variety of shrubs. What was he thinking of, coming way out here in the middle of nowhere to attend an interview. In fact, the advertisement in the newspaper was a little curious. The money to attend the interview – paid generously in advance for his expenses – was most acceptable.

They knew – whoever they were – all about him from his comprehensive application, but he knew nothing about them. Seeing this residence in its own grounds added something new to his anticipation.

Reaching the house, the driveway widened enough to allow cars turning space, then narrowed again, curving sharply and continuing in the direction of the rear of the building. He stopped in front of stone steps that led him between two marble pillars supporting a porch. A large oak door faced him with a heavy brass knocker.

There was no real need for him to take on another job immediately. He had put away a small nest-egg from his last employment. There hadn't been many chances to spend money on – in the back of beyond. Nearly everything was provided for him. On returning from abroad, he had seen an advert for a job vacancy, and almost without thinking applied to be considered.

Enthusiastic, industrious person required, capable of fact-finding research, and follow-up reports. The work will involve a fair amount of travelling. The position offers to the successful applicant, a good salary and accommodation if required for the length of employment. Send full details of work experience and any qualifications gained to: Box 472 Churchampton.

He wondered how many others had answered the advertisement, and how many would have wanted to fill the description they required.

It was not them who had advertised, but one man overrun with work by his success in undertaking research on an assortment of subjects. Henry Chorley answered the door. "Mr Davison, nice to meet you, good journey down?"

"Yes, thank you, very pleasant." They shook hands and Henry led Paul in to a room filled with books.

"For security reasons, the main gates are usually closed and locked throughout the day," he said apologetically. "This evening, I left them opened for you to drive in. Gates are opened only when we need to. All the family have keys. It's a bit of a nuisance unlocking and locking up when you go in and out of the grounds. There are reasons. A stranger was seen driving around the entire grounds on a couple of occasions. One of our daughters is a fashion model, and features in glossy magazines. Recently, she has had funny phone calls and bunches of flowers sent to her without the name of the sender. She has an uneasy feeling of being stalked. I thought I had to tell you as you might change your mind about working here."

Paul said, "It may be nothing, but worrying for you all. Thank you for telling me. No problem for me. It's very rare, but a stalker can have a harmless obsession or can be an extremely dangerous person."

"Unfortunately we don't know the type of person who is out there paying attention to her, or for what reason. There's some strange people about," Henry said warily.

"Have you informed the police?"

"Definitely, but they can do nothing without more proof."

Henry Chorley's pleasant manner gave Paul comfort when the interview started in earnest and progressed. He could offer work for about a year to start with, perhaps for years to come if the work kept coming in. He would be taken on probation for a while and if his work was satisfactory, permanently for as long as the work lasted.

Paul Davidson proved his worth. Ann Chorley was pleased to have a young man coming and going. If there were a stalker, he might think it was her daughter's young man that had come to stay, and leave her alone.

Breaks in life are rarely allocated fairly, and Paul Davidson's were no exception. An orphan that worked hard at his education, and found in travelling an agreeable substitute for his lack of home environment. His last job was with a group of archaeologists and helpers, who kept him employed for over two years. Although initially inexperienced in this field, with encouragement and training, helped quite adequately on their expedition abroad; working systematically to gently unearth artefacts with trowel, brush and a lot of patience in recording the finds made. For a young man of his age, Paul had had one or two girl friends, nothing serious or lasting. One day his hopes were to marry and put down roots, but at the moment, that seemed a long way off.

The time spent on the mission wasn't that long ago. On his ring finger of his left hand he wore a ring, given to him by a local man, for being in the right place at the right time. The circumstances involved a poisonous snake. Paul was talked through what had to be done; all he did really, was follow instructions. Without them he wouldn't have had a clue. The ring was a good piece of craftsmanship, many had admired the simple design, and even offered to buy it from him, unaware of the hidden potential it held. The ring was shaped in the form of a snake – which was an appropriate gift to give the young man as a reward. Its head, when pressed downwards against a spring clip, would enable it to be turned from side to front. This action would force a sharp needlepoint out of its mouth – barely visible. The needle had been coated with a diluted substance that the inhabitants used in the past, when hunting was the way of life in their existence. More than likely, the knowledge is still passed down from generation to generation.

Traditionally, in that part of the world, they repay their gratitude like for like, and so they gave Paul the ring. The gift ring could be worn as normal and also used as a defensive measure, if ever needed. The poison was capable of making a person unconscious for approximately half an hour; providing the needle scratched or pierced the skin, allowing the substance to get into the bloodstream. Paul had to accept the present, to refuse would have been an insult. He never imagined that it would ever be needed, or even if it would work after a long period of time.

All was going well, he liked his new job. One Saturday, time hung heavy. As soon as the doors opened at the village pub he would be there, he told himself. On leaving Chorley House to walk the road that led to the pub Paul was oblivious of three men, in a tan-coloured car, that showed interest in him. They were not far down the road. The first man pointed him out as he emerged alone from the side gate.

"What a stroke of luck, him showing his face! Not as though that it matters in any case, he's the only youngish man there," he told them, in confident manner.

The second man was heavily built. If you were to compare him with a commodity on sale in a shop, he would be placed in the knocked-down-price bin.

His looks were that of an ex-boxer who, despite his size, had met better in the ring. His nose at one time had been flattened, and it showed.

The third man was slim, gaudily dressed. His face displayed keen bird-like eyes. His chin protruded slightly.

The second man the Brawn, the third man, the Brains – that's how the first man viewed his companions; Brains and Brawn.

"You know what I want," the first man said.

"Leave it to us," Brains assured him. Brawn just grunted.

"Keep me posted," the first man insisted.

"It means a lot of hanging around without being conspicuous, not always easy these days," Brains emphasised. Brawn motioned agreement.

At that moment a blue sports car came along, flashing its headlights at Paul as it neared him. It was Leanne Chorley, the professional model.

She turned off the music cassette she was playing. "Hello," she said gaily. "Where are you off to?"

"For a bite to eat and a pint."

For a moment he thought she was going to drive on but she asked, "Mind if I join you? That sounds good."

"That would be nice, I'm not often seen with a beautiful model... but won't your parents be expecting you?"

"They won't mind, jump in – and as for beautiful models, you should see us when we first get out of bed in the morning, without our hair done and no make-up on, not a pretty sight," she said with laughter in her voice.

Paul got in the car and fastened his seat belt. "What sort of a week have you had?" he asked politely.

"Always busy in the fashion world... and you?" she enquired conversationally.

"Not too bad, just finished researching markings on a canon taken from a shipwreck by one of your father's clients."

"That sounds interesting," Leanne acknowledged.

She drove on a few yards or so where she found turning space. Leanne turned the car and headed back the way she had come.

The first man's face hardened. "They're pretty thick," he said frostily.

"Thicker than I thought." He then moodily turned the starter key of his car. After several manoeuvres in the road, he managed to point it in the opposite direction and drove off. Two miles on, the tan-coloured car stopped in a lay-by, letting Brains and Brawn out.

"There's no need to do too much hanging around, get on with the job.

"I'll up your fee," the first man growled.

"Can we ask why?" Brains tried his luck.

"That's personal," the other replied, sternly.

Brains and Brawn got in their own car, then both cars set off on their separate ways.

Paul and Leanne returned two hours later. Those two hours for Paul passed all too quickly. During those hours, she had let her feelings show more than at any other time he had briefly known her, and she wanted to know more about him. He found himself drawn to Leanne much closer. Exactly why, he couldn't understand.

She was unpredictable, beautiful, and successful. He hadn't at first given her a second thought, she was out of his league. Now, something within him was tugging at his heartstrings. True, she was attractive, but it wasn't that. Was the loneliness of his past catching up with him? This girl's company was at last telling him that travelling and job changes were not enough in his life. Should he dare contemplate that Leanne had any stronger feelings for him, other than this new friendliness she was showing towards him? She was used to a different way of life altogether. When she broke the news to him that it was not her intention to be stopping long, just a look in on the family as she had other plans, he accepted it without disappointment. She had other interests, others to be with, and that was that. It was none of his business. He could at least look on the bright side and live in hope.

That evening, Paul went again down to the village pub, content that company of sorts would be there. Perhaps a game of dominoes or darts with one or two of the locals. He remained at the pub until ten-thirty, finished his drink and made his way outside.

The winding road that was to take him back, was extremely dark. There were no street lights that one is accustomed to in towns. He walked briskly, keeping on grass verges close to the hedgerows and trees. He strode along on the right-hand side of the road, facing oncoming traffic should he meet any. He cursed himself for not wearing something light, to be seen plainly by any vehicle that might venture along this bending and potentially dangerous road at night. It was blacker now that he was out of sight of the pub's lights.

He was thankful that the driver coming up behind him was motoring with steady speed, with bright lights blazing. The car passed him carefully and slowly, then it stopped. The engine was turned off, the side and rear lights were kept on.

Two men got out of the front seats, slammed the doors and crossed the road to speak to him. They're lost and want to ask the way, Paul supposed. When they reached him, Brains spoke politely, cautiously and pleasantly: "You live at Chorley Manner don't you?"

"Yes," said Paul. "I do... how do you know that?"

Brawn said nothing, but edged nearer.

Ignoring the question and positive that they had the right man – by his own admission – Paul was in deep trouble. Before becoming aware of what was happening to him, he was in a vice-like grip from the bigger man, his arms were twisted painfully behind him and pushed up his back. He was manhandled bodily across the road to the nearside of the awaiting car, out of sight from any vehicle that might pass along this lonely stretch. Struggling to free himself proved useless. Brawn, still holding his arms firmly, spoke in his ear, breaking the silence since hauling Paul over the road. "You listen, my buddy don't like repeating 'imself."

Brains got close to Paul's face, knowing full well that his captive was powerless in the grip of the bigger man. The little man was cocky; the earlier pleasantry in his voice, lost. Speaking in a sarcastic tone, he said softly, "If you kick out, my friend will break both your arms. I'm easy-going, there is nothing personal in this you understand." With that he unmercifully punched him hard in the lower area of his body. Paul felt the agonising pain; then came another blow, much harder. For a moment he felt he was dying. The pain was unbearable, he found it hard to draw breath in his lungs. He felt sick, and his head reeled – Why are they doing this to me?

After what seemed hours to him, but in fact were only a minutes, the pain subsided to a bearable aching throb. Brains began speaking again in his chiding soft tone. "There won't be a mark on you. On the other hand... If you don't take my advice, and we have to talk to you again, my friend here is not so gentle. His marks will show up very badly. So be a good boy and keep away from Leanne Chorley, in fact why not be on the safe side and leave this area altogether."

So that's what it's all about. It wouldn't be so bad if she were his girlfriend, he was no threat to anyone, they were not that close. Would they believe him if he told them, he doubted that. Paul had never felt quite so angry with another person as he felt now. This smarmy little creep in front of him had to be brought down a peg or two. But how could he with 'Muscles' in attendance? Then, memory of his work abroad came rushing back to him – the ring. What could he do? Although his arms were held behind his back, his hands were free enough for him to touch his fingers. There must be no sudden movement. He located the head on his snake ring, pushed down very slowly and turned it from side to front. The sharp needle-like point, coated with a hunting preparation, emerged from its mouth. If only I can scratch the big fellow's skin. His mind raced. Will it be effective?

His ordeal came to an end. They appeared to have finished with him. He was no more than putty in their hands, they'd warned him and would be paid highly for doing so, by someone that needed a psychiatrist. They certainly weren't the stalkers. It was over as far as they were concerned.

The big man released his grip on Paul's arms. Paul began to sink gently to the grassy leaf-strewn verge, partly in weakness and partly with the idea of scratching some part of the big man's anatomy. As he sank nearer the ground, Brawn attempted to push Paul's body away from him with his foot. This was the opportunity. Clutching the big man's shoe with his right hand, as if warding off a kick, he slid his left hand up his trouser leg above the sock. Closing his fingers, he tore the needlepoint downwards on Brawn's bare flesh. For a few seconds he squatted, petrified, unsure what would happen. Would the big man kick out at him? He was unable to see the glassiness that came in the big man's eyes. In no time, Brawn's knees buckled and he fell slovenly to the ground; almost sprawling his big haunch on top of Paul. With great effort, Paul got to his feet, weak but anxious for confrontation with the man that had inflicted so much pain for a reason he wasn't guilty of.

Brains was in the process of leaving, to take his seat at the wheel of the car, taking for granted that Brawn would be following him, and that Paul would be left lying on the ground. Niggling questions flooded Paul's mind: How long would the big man be unconscious – for an average person, about half an hour he'd been told. For this man, who knows. How many times could the needle be used? In all probability only the once. Scuffing the point surely removed most of the coating.

He stood in the dim light that prevailed between the side and rear lamps of the car. Brains' complacency became shattered by disbelief in finding Paul standing upright in front of him.

"Now we are one to one," Paul rasped, driven on by pent-up emotion. "Who the hell sent you? and what difference does it make whether I see her or not! I'm not her boyfriend, you idiot."

The beating, began to make sense. That is if you can make sense of people with warped minds and to pay others to do your dirty work.

"What the... Frank!... Frank!" Brains used the big fellow's name for the first time and realised there would be no help. Brawn lay immobile on the ground.

The little man was panicky, mystified by not being able to understand what had happened to the protector of his loud mouth. His confidence faded away and he broke out in a cold sweat.

Paul wanted answers and wanted them fast, but was given no time. He half saw and half sensed Brains' hands fumbling in his pockets. What was he fumbling for? a knife? He wasn't about to wait to find out. He hit Brains on the chin with the full force of his left clenched fist. The needle on the ring was still bared. Brains fell like a log. Paul wasn't certain whether it had anything to do with traces of substance still remaining on the point, or the hard blow he had struck, or a mixture of both that had floored him.

Whatever it was, there was no time to gloat; he must act quickly. These boys didn't play the game to 'Queensbury' rules, and he didn't intend to hang around longer than necessary. Putting his hands under Brains' armpits, he pulled him close in to the hedgerow, sitting him upright with his knees under his chin. He was light in weight and easily moved. Paul undid the shoelace on his right shoe and

70

removed the shoe from his foot. He flung it as hard as he could over the hedgerow and into the field beyond. He did the same with his sock. The big fellow was a different proposition, a much greater challenge to move. He was far too heavy to manoeuvre in the same way. After removing his left shoe and sock and flinging them both in the opposite field, rolled him over. It wasn't easy, his body still hurting from the blows. Having achieved this with satisfaction, he took a small notebook from his pocket and tore out a page. He hastily scribbled:

> *You'll find your car in front of Chorley House. Have a nice walk. Think yourselves lucky this time, I could have ended your useless lives.*

Paul grinned, as he tied the note on Brains' wrist with his flashy tie.

He got in their car and quickly drove it to the gates of Chorley House and left it with its parking lights on, and key in the ignition. He let himself in through the side gate with his key that Henry Chorley had given him when he hired him. The walk back to his cosy room in his temporary home, was an effort. The driveway seemed twice as long to cover at half pace. When he eventually reached the stairway, every step up made him wince. What a predicament. He briefly felt that he should never have got involved with the Chorley family, having been so painfully warned off. He let himself into his room, and dropped onto the bed, lying there relaxing every muscle in his body. A self-satisfied grin appeared on his face. He thought; I wonder if they'll walk to their car together, with one shoe off and one shoe on. Or, will they have sense enough for the big fellow to give the smaller man his other shoe. That way, only he need come for the car, whilst the other waits to be picked up in relative comfort."

The young man never found out. All he learned the next morning was that the car had gone. He could only speculate what the two thugs had said or done to the one possessing paranoid delusions, and obsessions. They must have believed when they came back to consciousness – and reading his note – that Paul could have ended their lives.

Leanne received no more unwanted phones calls or flowers. Paul was never approached again by the two thugs. Ann and Henry Chorley were pleased that the stalking had stopped, and that Leanne and Paul went out together occasionally whenever both their work permitted.

The big gates to the grounds, are now open all day again.

*   *   *

Birdwatcher

There are numerous sayings that are still very popular, one that comes to mind is, *'A Liar is worse than a Thief.'* Some would dispute this and possibly reverse the saying. You can make a loss from both the thief and a liar, depending on what he's lying about. A recent happening made me dwell on the differences.

Tom Haddon, now retired, worked for many years as a teacher of sign language and lip reading for the deaf and dumb. He had become quite an expert in this field of teaching with so many years of experience. After retirement he took up the hobby of bird watching. One early morning he went to a wooded area and began to examine the region closely through his binoculars. As he moved the field glasses in search of wildlife, he focussed on two men who were sitting on a pile of logs. Tom Haddon became nosey and began to read their lips for a bit of fun. One of the men was smoking a pipe and spoke at times with it in his mouth, and Tom could not fully understand all he was saying while he had the pipe between his lips. The other man he understood easily.

Their conversation shocked Tom. The non-smoker said: "They've been away now for three days. No one has been to the house. It is unlikely there is a pet to be fed by the look of it, which makes it that much easier. When can you do the job?"

The smoker spoke with his pipe still in his mouth, his answer Tom believed to be, 'Thursday,' and made out plainly, 'anyone else?'

"No, there's only me and you that know. I'm not fool enough to tell anyone else. It is a secluded house so you shouldn't have any trouble. You should find some high-quality valuables there." He went on to give the address.

The pipe smoker jotted it down. With that they both got up and moved away.

When Tom Haddon informed the police of the information he'd gathered in the woods, they didn't believe him. They thought he was a trifle eccentric and wasting police time. It did not seem feasible that this man could put together a plausible conversation through a pair of binoculars, and that he'd got it all wrong.

"By the look on your faces, you think I'm some kind of nut. If you're not content, check my teaching credentials," Tom said, most annoyed.

When eventually the police learned of Tom Haddon's background, they took him seriously and laid in wait for the attempted burglary. Focusing particularly on the Thursday that Tom Haddon had thought he made out the day to be.

It took a lot of police resources, but it eventually paid off. Two men arrived in an unnamed furniture van, and immediately forced their way into the premises. The police hung back for a while until the thieves put a few of the owner's belongings into the van. Then they moved in and made their arrest.

Tom Haddon was summoned to identify the culprits as the two men in the woods who planned the whole thing.

"I can identify one. He is the person that was smoking a pipe. The other man I've not seen before," Tom said earnestly.

The police were not happy, they had not got in custody all those involved. There had been similar burglaries in the past, in and around that area, and it left loose ends. If they didn't get the organiser, the burglaries would continue they figured.

The police interviewed the two men, attempting to find the other man who was in the woods with the pipe smoker.

"I don't know who 'e is… I was brought in to help at the last moment," said the man Tom couldn't identify.

The Inspector in charge of the proceedings turned his attention to the pipe smoker. He had to be very diplomatic and not tell direct lies to those in custody for fear of the charge of gaining information under false pretences, which might weaken his case. He would bend the truth to get the other man who was still at large. He looked at the pipe-smoking man and commented:

"You obviously have a collaborator, is that not so?"

"No, I work entirely on my own," he lied.

"You don't expect me to believe that, you must have been tipped off that the occupants of this house were away on holiday."

"That's your problem, not mine," he smugly answered.

"I dare say you'd like to know, how we knew you'd be there at that particular time, and be in waiting for you."

"That's what's been puzzling me," the pipe smoker replied glumly. "I doubt very much you are about to tell me."

"No, I cannot divulge the source. Work it out for yourself, you were told only he and you knew the details of the location. It only takes one anonymous phone call you know," the Inspector remarked cautiously, not saying precisely whether he had an anonymous call or not.

"Flipping heck, you are right, that was said to me. It must have been him who tipped you off... no one else knew of that, you had to be there to know what was said. But why should he have done that. It makes no ruddy sense."

The Inspector didn't have to tell the pipe-smoking man that it wasn't him that gave the accurate information. "Are you prepared to give us his name?" the Inspector asked.

"Too damned right I am – if I knew it. The conniving bugger. What have I done to upset him, that's what I want to know. What I do know is that he works in a Travel Agents and knows exactly when people go away on holiday and for how long. He passes the information on to me. We always meet in the same spot in the woods, no names mentioned. Normally I do the jobs myself. This time I got Jack to give me a hand with the loading into the van because the house is much larger than I'm used to tackling and more to be shifted. It's always worked nicely up to now. I wouldn't be a bit surprised in thinking he thought I was double-crossing him and flogging off some of the goods behind his back and not giving him his full cut. That's for me to know and him to find out. He didn't think me smart enough to fathom out who tipped you off. Well he's got another think coming."

"Where did you first meet the man?" the Inspector asked.

"In a pub," the other replied. "We got talking, and that's how it all started."

The Inspector needed nothing more from the detainees.

All the police had to do now was to ask the house owner what travel agent he'd booked his holiday with. Tom Haddon would accompany them to the travel agent named, and be able to recognise the employee. The case would be solved.

Thieves, liars and truth benders. In this case, truth bending done in the name of justice.

* * *

Planet Earth

The spacecraft neared the planet Earth. "It's beautiful," the second-in-command said to his captain. "It's even more beautiful when we get close enough to see the golden and green fields, the blue and green waters, the wonderful trees and colourful flowers, the hills and valleys, the mountains, the lakes. Truly a magnificent sight, but there is much evil on this planet... Of course, this is your first time here, isn't it?"

"Yes, I am privileged to be chosen."

The captain frowned. "Our forefathers have been studying this planet for thousands of years. Little has changed in attitude by these Earthlings. Somewhere down there they will be killing one another. There are many good Earthlings, but they appear to be outnumbered by the greedy and power-seeking kind. Even in parts of this planet where there is democracy, they still rob and murder and make life difficult to be lived in comfort. There's no point in a country gaining democracy if it is replaced by a corrupt government. I will not go into too much detail of the cruelty and sheer wickedness that goes on, to talk about it can be very disturbing."

"Have we ever landed or contacted these Earthlings?"

"One of our craft unwisely left markings in corn fields. They had no authority to do so. Luckily enough some Earthlings copied what we had done and it is believed to be of their own making and not ours. They call the patterns in the fields 'Crop Circles'. We have been recording the hundreds of different languages and dialects from all over this planet and feeding them into our computers. We are at the stage now that we are able to understand most of them. We must only hover for a short space of time in order not to be seen clearly, unfortunately we have been spotted briefly. Those that have spotted us and told others, are not believed by the majority, and are themselves uncertain and cannot be sure of what they've witnessed and therefore there is no proof that we exist. These Earthlings have some strange customs that we cannot fully understand even now. Twenty-two men kick a bag of wind about for an hour and a half. They call this football. Another thing they do is throw a ball and another hits it with a piece of wood and they chase the ball. They call this cricket. The strangest I find is fishing, when one of them sits or stands by water with a piece of string on a stick and waits for hours with the string dangling in the water. It seems such a waste of time to catch a fish."

The captain paused but wanted to give more information. "We have been accused by a tiny minority that we have kidnapped a few of them and studied them on board our spacecrafts. This we could not do for fear of putting our own planet at risk by bringing back many of the bacteria and diseases that are on this planet. That is why we will never land. We are only here to observe. When they see something in the sky they do not understand they call them UFOs – Unidentified Flying Objects. They even call us Flying Saucers. The more advanced nations here have come a long way in technology. They have been able to put a spaceship on the moon and walked on its surface, but that is only a mere 238857 miles from Earth." He paused again, and had a drink.

"They can send probes out to outer space. They have the atom and nuclear bombs and weapons of mass destruction that have the potential of destroying all forms of life on the planet. One day in the future they may well blow themselves to pieces if they are not mindful of what they are doing."

"They are not as advanced as us. Surely we have nothing to fear from them, have we?" said his second-in-command, questioningly.

"That's the only reason why we keep an eye on them. To see how far they are progressing. We've little to concern ourselves at the moment, they have a long way to go to get anywhere near our technology. We never will reach the speed of light of 186000 miles per second, but we do speed a tiny fraction of the light scale. Our only fear from these Earthlings is, if ever they reach our planet, will they come in peace or be hostile to us. They cannot trust each other on Earth, so how can we put our trust in them. No, we cannot do that. I don't think they will ever get near to our planet; we will continue to observe and never contact them. They are composed of a different substance than us, and hopefully will never be able to reach the speeds we travel at. At this point in time, their bodies would never survive in the spacecraft they have. Let's make one more circumnavigation of this world, then go home. By then I will have seen and recorded all I want on this mission for the time being."

With that in mind, they would make their way back to planet Quarus, to report and express possibly the view that there'll be no need for another visit for a couple of decades.

On Earth, a man and his wife were walking their dogs down a country lane. The wife looked up at the sky and caught a glimpse of the spacecraft departing speedily. "Look! Quick! Charlie," she shrilled. "Up there, look!"

He looked up but there was nothing to be seen. "What?" he asked.

"It looked like one of them Flying Saucers," she gasped.

"I know you thought you saw a Flying Saucer, dear, but I think there is quite a perfectly reasonable explanation for these sightings. It might be a reflection from something. A mirage perhaps. Optical phenomenon... You know the type of thing; reflection or refraction of light. Like the heat rising from the sand in the desert. You see an oasis from a distance, and when you reach the spot where you thought you saw it, there's nothing there, non-existent. Just think of what's up in the atmosphere – planes, balloons, probes, satellites, space stations and goodness knows what else there is going around the Earth. If there were little green men from outer space, after all this time that people said they've seen them, surely they would have made contact with us by now. No, I don't believe there's anything out there. I'd put money on it."

* * *

Trust no one

The day started like any other for the man seated in a First Class compartment on the early morning train. At one of the stations stopped at along the way, a man in a dark suit joined him in the compartment and sat opposite him. The newcomer appeared to be about 50 years old and the first man noticed that he wore a vicar's collar.

The newcomer was the first to speak: "Good morning," he said and smiled at the same time.

"Good morning to you, Vicar, and a nice one it is too."

After a short space of time the vicar said softly, "The Bishop would not like to hear me say this, but trust no one. I have had one of the most nasty con tricks pulled on me. It is my own fault; I am too trusting for my own good you see, being one of the drawbacks of my profession. Unfortunately, with one's calling to God, I need to have trust and faith in my fellow mankind. It's not as if I wasn't forewarned. It was pointed out on the television not that long ago, to be aware of such things."

The other man looked concerned. "What exactly happened then?" he asked.

"Let me introduce myself; I am the Reverend Leslie Smyth, and you are? if I may ask."

"My name is George Vandenburg, and my work is in Stocks and Shares."

"There are so many con tricks in circulation, it's unbelievable. You are at a supermarket about to get a trolley. Someone comes up to you with their trolley that they are about to return, and says: 'to save you bother, give me your pound and take this one.' You give them a pound coin and do your shopping. When you return to get the pound coin out that you believe the other person put in, you find that they had a way of removing their coin before offering the trolley to you."

"Is that what happened in your case then, Vicar?" Vandenburg asked, slightly amused and holding back a chuckle with difficulty.

"Oh no, nothing so trivial. I'm just pointing out some of the dirty tricks people get up to. I was speaking to a person working in one of the big DIY stores, and he told me about one of the scams used there: It was to select an item in a large cardboard box, with say something inside that was wanted by the shopper, and whilst going up and down the aisles they would craftily put into the box, smaller valuable items. When eventually they get to the checkout counter, the box only is the object priced and paid for, and of course all that is inside, is unpaid for."

Vandenburg looked across at him with faint curiosity, hoping he would come to the point but the other man continued along the same lines: "Everyone naturally by now knows of the two bogus water company employees who call at your front door saying there is a burst pipe or some other excuse to get into your house. One keeps you occupied downstairs while the other supposedly checks your taps upstairs and steals any valuables he finds. People still fall for this old trick. Schoolchildren, and some warped adults as well, come up to you in the street and say that they have lost their money and could you give them the bus fare home. One woman said she had had her handbag stolen. You kindly oblige and it is not until you see them doing the same thing to someone else that you realise you've been conned and you feel very angry at being such a fool."

"This is the way you've been hoodwinked is it?" Vandenburg put forward.

"No, no, if it was only as minor as a bus fare, I would have nothing to complain about."

"Then what is it then that is troubling you?" Vandenburg demanded in a quiet inoffensive tone of voice.

"I never draw money from cash machines... never. I go once a month to get a statement, that's all. At the end of last month I went along as usual to one of these machines. As I approached I noticed a young lady to my left. When I got close to the machine, a young gentleman came up and stood behind me. I use the word 'gentleman' loosely. Well, as I put my card in the contraption, he distracted me by saying; 'Is that your purse on the floor?' I looked down to find an old purse. No, I said. He picked it up. He opened it and said, 'It's empty, not worth taking it to the police station.' I turned to continue with my transaction. My card as I thought had been taken in by the machine, so I fed my personal identification number in, but nothing happened. 'Having trouble?' he asked. 'Yes,' I said. 'Try again,' he suggested. I fed my PIN number in again without success. He left immediately because he was not going to trust putting his card in after what had happened to mine, was his excuse for leaving. Of course all this was untrue, knowing what I know now."

At this point the ticket collector came and checked their tickets. Satisfied that they had paid First Class fares he quickly left them.

"Now where was I, ah, yes… It was a scam of course. He distracted me, the timing was perfect. As I looked down at the purse on the floor, his accomplice took my card from the machine before it was taken in. He naturally looked over my shoulder and noted my PIN number. Before I could get the card stopped at the bank they had drawn £200 from my account. So I say again, trust no one."

"I'm sorry to hear of the loss about anyone who is robbed, let alone a man of the church," said Vandenburg sympathetically.

"That's the way of the world I'm afraid. I get out at the next station, nice to have passed the time of day with you, young man."

As the train slowly pulled in, the vicar stood up and lost his balance and fell awkwardly onto Vandenburg.

"I'm so terribly sorry, please excuse my clumsiness," he said apologetically.

"That's quite alright, no harm done I'm sure," said Vandenburg. "Just one moment, there is some white chalky powder on your shoulder." He stood up and brushed it off. "There, that's better," he remarked with satisfaction.

The train came to a halt and the vicar got off. Two men also alighted at the same time.

Vandenburg continued his journey to the city but did not go directly to his place of work. Instead he went to Police Head Quarters to meet his friend – Chief Inspector Jarvis. The detective greeted him cordially and offered him a seat and sent for coffee. "Shouldn't have long to wait, depending on the traffic," he said.

The wait was longer than expected, it was a good hour before the two that followed the vicar from the train arrived. By their side stood the Reverend Smyth.

"You found my wallet on him then?" asked Vandenburg.

Smyth was shocked. "You are a policeman then are you? How on earth did you know? I've been so careful. I have principles, I only take from those that can afford it. Always from them in First Class compartments... This is entrapment!"

"No, I'm not a policeman," answered Vandenburg. "My friend here is Chief Inspector Jarvis who is aware that I travel every day on this city line, and repeatedly had complaints by passengers of being robbed over the last few years. He asked if I would for a short time carry a microchip sensor pin that is traceable by experienced officers. Because of the cost of having policemen close by me on the train, it could only be tried for a short time; just a few weeks. The police were fortunate that you picked on me this morning. No, I did not trap you. You have taken an ordinary businessman's wallet from his pocket, with my money, bank cards and with a genuine name and address. No, this is not entrapment, you chose to take it from me. You were very good, but I can't believe that you are, or ever were a vicar. I was informed that the person doing the stealing would normally brag of his exploits but act as the victim. This is your Achilles heel, you can't stop yourself. When I pretended to brush something off your shoulder, I actually inserted the sensor pin."

The bogus vicar said: "You are so right, my clever travelling companion. I can't help talking about the things I've done in my lifetime – and got away with until now – and the police here will never be able to prove any of it." He laughed heartily. "I should have taken my own advice... Trust no one."

* * *

Dream On

Royalty, naturally, have a completely different lifestyle than the rest of us. Being human, their emotions however are exactly the same; feeling pain, disappointment, happiness and sadness, as we all experience from time to time during our lifetime. Always in the public eye 24 hours a day has its drawbacks, and some ambitions and desires are almost impossible to fulfil. Most people would not find this way of life enticing and in no way give up their own privacy to be a member of the royal family.

The Queen had for many years a burning desire to mix unrestricted socially – even if only for a few hours – with one or two of the general public. She would have liked the experience of having those she met not having to curtsey or bow every time they were in front of her, to be treated as an ordinary person and not for people to be on guard of what they say for fear of giving offence. To get away from protocol for a short time would be wonderful. An almost unattainable objective to accomplish.

She expressed these inner feelings one day to her friend and confidant, Lady Jane, "I would very much like to walk the streets of London on my own for an hour or two. To be able to buy myself an ice cream from a vender, to go in a café and order an 'All-day-Breakfast' or something. To speak to people without restricting them and get their true opinions. In other words I would like to be just one of the crowd. Perhaps I could try my hand at catching a bus to somewhere not too far away. I've never had the simplicity and pleasure of buying a bus ticket, which is very sad."

Lady Jane shrugged her shoulders and looked shocked. "You cannot be serious, Your Majesty. If you truly mean what you are saying, that is entirely out of the question, the Prime Minister and Parliament would never hear of such a thing – let alone your family. The prestige of your position that you have so perfectly upheld all these years has to be maintained. The dedication and service you have given to your country over these many years is unquestionable. It would be for the very first time that you have no one to look out for your safety and well-being. You would have to cross the road, using a pedestrian crossing. A thing you have never done in your life. You could be knocked down and killed by a car. What a field day the papers would have with that. There's always a possibility of being attacked by a thug in an attempt to steal from you. There are far too many dangers for any person not being streetwise… or come to that, even if you are streetwise, the dangers are still there. It is unreasonable to believe in any case, that you could be received by anyone you meet as not being the Queen. Your face is on every banknote and coin in the country and regularly in the newspapers and on television. Your smart clothes are a giveaway of your wealth and importance. It is improbable to be anything other than who you are. What you seek is out of reach. There is so much that is different in ordinary life. I'm not saying you could not do these things if you were brought up that way. I am aware your duties are very demanding that you undertake now. The run of the mill person has to hold down a full-time job as well as shopping, cooking, washing up, cleaning, ironing, bed making and so on and so on. You were born to be Queen with no alternative," Lady Jane emphasized strongly.

The Queen understood what she was saying, persisting with her own thoughts. "The family members are away for a long weekend, Polo games and attending Goodwood and a few other personal commitments to be taken care of. I'll be on my own. This gives me the ideal opportunity. If I don't do it now at my age, I never will. You could help me to achieve what I want if you have the bravado to do so. It would be so different, and for once in my lifetime a solo adventure."

"How is that possible? I would be shunned if it was found out that I'd helped in such a precarious scheme. My position in society would be permanently ruined and in tatters if anything unforeseen happened to you," Lady Jane retorted apprehensively.

"I will write a note exonerating anyone from blame for my absence from the palace for the time I am away," the Queen said. "Take it as a command if you wish, this is what I want you to do; first of all go to one of those charity clothes shops that I've heard of and buy me an outfit that I can use that will obviously not be too smart. I need a darkish wig for extra disguise. Perhaps sunglasses, a false nose even. I will require some money to spend – I've never done that before. How exciting!"

"If you do this and it all goes wrong, they will put two and two together that someone had to help you. They would want to know who brought these items that you asked for, into the palace."

After the Queen's reassurance that she would not be implicated, Lady Jane reluctantly obeyed, but hoped she would never go through with such a plan. She was wrong. The following day the Queen changed into her new guise and went out through the staff entrance onto the London streets, promising Lady Jane she would only be gone for a short while, and not to worry. She was quite capable of looking after herself. She signed a security pass to be able to leave and re-enter the palace as one of the Queen's personal guests.

It was a very strange feeling for the Queen walking along and passing people who never gave her a second glance. No waving of flags and cheering. She queued up with some over excited, noisy, and not too polite children to buy an ice cream. When it was her turn to be served, the seller had a laugh and a joke with her, which she thoroughly enjoyed. She was amused when he asked, "Wada you want, love?" After being served she made her way along the road licking her ice cream cornet as she did so, smiling to herself as she went. It felt as if a weight had been lifted from her head leaving the responsibly of being Queen behind her, knowing full well it would only be for a short while – she would make the most of it. The sun broke through the clouds. She went and sat on a bench in St. James's Park and listened to everyday conversations as the public strolled by. One or two swear words were heard, she grinned and took no offence, she'd heard worse on the television.

No one paid the slightest attention to her, no one so far had recognised her. She was full of joy. Deciding not to venture on a bus, as time passed so quickly, the next call she made was at a café off the main road, where she wanted to experience the eating of plain cooking. She opened the door and peeped in. There were about twenty others seated in not too a generous space between them. She sat down inconspicuously at a vacant table by the window. She had to wait patiently for some time before she was seen and given a menu. She looked through what was on offer and ordered a meat and vegetable meal with a pot of tea. When she had finished picking over the food – to her dissatisfaction – Sally the waitress came.

"Everything OK, dear? Anything else?" the waitress asked politely.

"No, not really," the Queen said, "the meat was just about acceptable but I thought the vegetables were overcooked and had no flavour. I didn't like them at all. This cloth on the table is not especially clean. There are a few stains."

Sally left her and shortly afterwards returned with the bill. The Queen paid the exact amount. The waitress went without comment.

Shortly afterwards the waitress returned to the kitchen with dirty dishes and to collect meals that had been ordered earlier by other customers.

When the door was safely closed behind her and out of earshot, she said to the chef, "Some old dear out there has not been very complimentary, Fred, and I didn't get a tip."

"Why, what's wrong?"

"The old dear remarked the tablecloth is grubby, and thinks your cooking is overcooked and tasteless."

The chef became annoyed at once, the words hurting his pride.

"Damned fussy, isn't she. Who the hell do she think she is, The Queen!"

* * *

The Gold-framed Mirror

Ian Gwynn with his wife Shirley and two children, Terry and Debbie, moved into their new home in the country a week before Christmas. All the furniture was neatly arranged and the last job that was done was fitting a large gold-framed mirror over the mantelpiece. All appeared to be going well and on Christmas Eve they decorated the living room with coloured chains and placed the presents around the Christmas tree. On Christmas morning Ian was first up and started to comb his hair in front of the mirror. Something was wrong. The reflection of the room's contents were entirely different. Surely he hadn't bought a duff distorted mirror?

He looked behind him in disbelief. Mystified he turned and looked in the mirror again. The decorations were dissimilar, the tree was nothing like his own, and the fairy lights were larger. A chill ran down his spine and the hairs at the back of his neck stood up. He blinked and looked once more, still the same. He quickly moved away rubbing his eyes and waited for his wife to get up and come into the room.

"Have a glance in the mirror and tell me if you see anything unusual, Shirley," he suggested nervously, hoping she would see the same as he had seen.

She came over to the mirror slightly bemused, and looked at her face. "No, I'm just as beautiful without my make-up," she said with a big smile.

"No, no, the reflection of the room's contents," he explained.

She looked again in the mirror. "You must have started drinking early," she laughed. "Take more water with it. I can't see anything that's out of place. What are you on about for goodness sake?"

"Well it must be my bleary eyes," he said, not wanting to go into detail or make a complete fool of himself. There had to be a simple explanation.

She left the room and went to the kitchen to prepare the festive meals.

When she was out of sight he looked in the mirror again; it had not changed since the last time he had looked. This was frightening. Was he going mad? He put his finger softly on the glass and his finger went through into the unreal reflected room. The next thing he was aware of was a hand pulling him gently all the way through. He felt as light as a feather until his feet landed firmly on the floor. He looked around him, terrified, but was drawn by some unknown force to calmly go to the other rooms of the house. This was against his will but he could not stop the compelling force. The rooms were exactly the same as his own, only differently furnished with photographs of a family unknown to him. He found himself at the front door of the house but would not dare to go out under any circumstances. He glanced out of the window in the door, again the garden was the same except for rose beds and not lawn. It felt to him as if he'd been transported back in time.

Suddenly, the ghostly figure of an attractive young lady appeared and stood in front of him. The calmness he had felt, vanished, and he started to shiver. Was this some horrible nightmare?

"Christmas is supposed to be a wonderful family time of the year," she said sadly, "but a tragedy struck one Christmas morning years ago in this house. You have given me my chance to join my beloved family by just being here. I have been longing for someone with a large gold-framed mirror – the same as ours – to make it all happen for me, Christmas past to Christmas present. No questions please, I beg of you. I could not bear to speak about it, but I know now that the waiting's over and that happiness will soon be mine. Please pardon my motives for putting you through this unwanted occurrence in your life. Beware, you have only this morning to make it back through the mirror to your own surroundings, otherwise you will have to wait for another Christmas morning and hope the mirror is still in its place. There must be no other person's reflection in the mirror when you go back through. Go quickly! Please forgive me, there was no other way."

He moved as fast as his legs could carry him to reach the mirror. Checking the room to see that his children or his wife were not in there, he climbed back. He gave out a cry of overwhelming relief when his feet touched the floor. He could not resist the temptation to look in the mirror once more. He thanked God all he saw was the genuine reflection of his own room.

Shirley was still in the kitchen, the children occupied in their bedrooms. He would say nothing to anyone – not even his wife – of his eerie and frightening experience, because it could never be proven or explained in this world, and no one would believe him anyhow. Strangers or family would come to the conclusion that he was going off his rocker – or that he'd turned into a compulsive liar – if he breathed a word of it.

The Gwynn family spent a most enjoyable Christmas together, with no other distractions – except for a mysterious "Thank you" on one of their Christmas decorated napkins, which seemed inappropriate to all but one.

Ian had no fear now of looking in the gold-framed mirror, and it wasn't until the New Year that he felt the compelling urge to find out something about that family and the tragedy that followed – *the when, the where and the why*. The *where* had to be the house they were now living in, otherwise he wouldn't have had the frightening experience. He would look at the deeds, and try to find that family who lived there, and most essential to come across a name. He could then go and search through old newspapers at the News Centre. The back copies of papers are now computerised, it would be much easier than manually turning page after page.

The task needed a lot of thought.

The next day he went and collected the deeds that were in safe keeping at the bank. Obviously, it wasn't the couple he'd bought the house from. Working backwards from them was a foreigner, with a name hard to pronounce. He continued to search and found that ten years ago the house was sold one February. If it had been sold in say November, it couldn't have been the family he was looking for. He wrote down the name of 'Wallace' and would go to the News Centre the following day. Hoping he'd got it right, otherwise it would be back to the drawing board.

It took him ages scrolling through the news items. He almost gave up a couple of times, to come back another day. My eyes are tired and feeling as watery as weak beer, he told himself. And then, as he viewed another page, there it was – husband and children found dead, the wife rushed to hospital but passed away two days later. The report gave the area but, intentionally, not the house. He could hardly see what he was reading; he was straining his eyes, but he must read on. A basket with a few remnants of deadly fungus – that could be mistaken for mushrooms – was found in their kitchen. The reading shed no light on who picked them from the woods. Apparently, they had eaten them fried, with eggs and bacon for breakfast. There was much more to read but Ian had found what he'd come for. The newspapers were not able to say who picked the fungus, but Ian knew that it had to be Mrs Wallace, that's why her soul could not rest. She'd suffered the horrible guilt for ending all their lives prematurely, for not knowing what she was doing. Family souls kept apart, longing for the time of being together again. It was such a tragic story. He would rest his eyes. It was now all reasonably clear to him. There was nothing more he wanted his mind to be burdened with.

He drove home and parked his car.

As he entered the house, Shirley said, "Where on earth have you been, you're late! I'm beginning to think you've got another woman on the go."

"You've got to be joking, I couldn't manage two. What's for dinner? I'm starving."

"That's all you think about, your belly. Now let me see, we have cottage pie followed by sherry trifle... Oh, and yes, as a treat for a starter, I've made a wild mushroom soup."

*   *   *

Leave Well Alone

Marc Denham drove slowly along the main road looking for Harwood Avenue. It came into view. It was a turning on his right. He flashed his indicator and turned when able to do so. He was pleased not to see double yellow lines, permit buying or parking meters. It made him annoyed that car owners paid road tax and, at every opportunity, efforts were made by local councils to extract more and more money from the motorist – they knew damned well they had to stop and park their cars somewhere. Parking meters must be breeding like flies, he thought, they appeared to be popping up all over the damn place.

He drove at a crawling pace gazing at both sides of the road for number 203. Finding it on the left-hand side, he stopped in front of it, and got out of the car. He stood there for a while taking in the surrounds, then he walked up the path to the front door. In the window to his right a large sign read 'Vacancies'. Marc rang the doorbell and waited. In no time at all it was answered by a woman, who in her younger years must have been very attractive – judging by her features, he thought. She looked at him and simply inquired, "Yes?"

"Good morning," Marc said, "I'm up here on business for a few days and hope you can put me up."

She ran her eyes quickly over him, "Please come in."

After he entered she closed the door behind him and led him into the front room.

"How long is it you want to stay?" she asked pleasantly.

"I'm not absolutely sure, but it won't be any less than four days," he said, "I've several clients to see."

"You're in luck. It's quite a large house, but we only let out four rooms. At the moment, we have just a young lady and a middle-aged gent staying with us. I'll take you up and show you a room – if you want it, we can offer breakfast or an evening meal as well, it's whatever suits you. The price is payable in advance – I'm sorry, nothing personal, but you know how things are in today's world."

"Don't I know it, I could tell you a few things," Marc said with a smile.

She took him to one of the vacant rooms upstairs. It was very clean and tidy. It had a chair and somewhere he could put his laptop computer on, if he needed to do some work in the room. He was more than pleased. When they were downstairs again he decided to have full board, and paid the amount she quoted, and was told of the times the meals would be served, and if it suited him, which it did.

She gave him the key to his room. "For my paperwork, can I have your name and address Mr…?" she asked.

"Marc Denham, but please call me Marc." He then gave her his address which she wrote down.

"By the way, what shall I call you Mrs…?" He was deceptive, he already knew her name.

"The name is Mathews. Just call me Irene, the other guests do. May I ask what you do for a living Mr… er Marc?"

"I work for Harlow, Harlow and Mason, solicitors a lot of the time. Nothing grand but I do a little detective work for them. Don't be alarmed I'm only on discrete private investigating. I'm not carrying a gun as they do in America. Nothing I do you could call dangerous," he laughed.

"How did you come to be wanting to stay here? Were we recommended by someone that had stayed with us before?"

"No, I was driving by after leaving a client and noticed your sign," he lied. "If it's alright with you, I'll collect my suitcase from the car and settle in my room for a while. I won't be up there long, I have to meet someone about a suspected fraudulent claim."

"Oh," she said, without further comment.

"I have to do a lot of driving in the next few days but this place is nice and central. I'll see you this evening and look forward to meeting your other guests. I'll go on up then."

"Take your time, Marc."

"Thanks."

He left her, collected his suitcase and went to his room. Marc was out of the house and on his way 20 minutes later, the main reason why he came there uppermost in his mind.

That evening Marc returned to the guest house and was let in by Mr Mathews.

"Hello," he said, "I'm Irene's husband John, you must be Marc, our new guest."

"Pleased to meet you," Marc replied. "If you don't mind me asking, have you any grown-up children living with you? Your wife never mentioned any, only the other guests."

"We have a daughter and two grandchildren. Our daughter hasn't lived here for many years, she's living up in Scotland with her husband and family."

"Sorry," Marc said, "I didn't mean to sound nosey."

"No offence taken, Marc, nice to have an enquiring mind in your business." He gave Marc a broad smile. Irene must have mentioned to her husband what Marc did for a living.

They made small talk for a while then Marc made his way up to his room, showered and changed his shirt. When he came down for the evening meal, both the other guests along with Mr and Mrs Mathews were sitting down in the lounge, chatting. When he entered the room they all stood up and greeted him warmly. Introductions were made.

"You've met my husband John. This is Stanley Bartoc," Irene said, "and this is Sharon Vaughn."

They both shook his hand, then they all went into dining room for their evening meal and got to know one another a little better with amiable conversation.

Although Marc at times had to ask direct questions, he had a knack of getting to know from others, by just saying what had happened to him in a particular place or on mentioning a certain subject, and found people voluntarily coming out with their own experiences, giving him what he wanted to hear concerning them – but not always.

On the second day at the evening meal, he remarked, "If I were running this big place, I would certainly need help with all of the effort that has to go into it."

Irene said, "My husband and I do most of the work, but Sheila Brown comes in three afternoons a week to help out."

The information may not be of any use to him, but Marc learned of another person associated with that address without asking.

The following days he was there were pleasant. They all seemed – on the surface – to be nice people, easy to get along with. Stanley Bartoc worked for a computer firm and was quite talkative. Sharon Vaughn was not so informative to Marc, and seemed as though she had something she didn't want revealed, perhaps eyeing him with suspicion because of the work he did.

He felt now that by staying any longer, would not alter the situation that had brought him there. He'd taken care of all the business side for the solicitors and other clients. On the morning of his last day after breakfast, he packed his suitcase and brought it downstairs. Mrs Mathews was found in the kitchen.

"I'm ready for the off, and thank you for a very enjoyable stay. It could not have been better," he said truthfully.

"Thank you very much, and if you are up here on business again, you know where we are."

Marc hesitated, "Are we able to have a word in complete privacy, without being disturbed?"

"They are all at out, no one will be back this morning," she said mystified.

"I was about to leave without saying a word, but my conscience tells me otherwise. I've not been straightforward with you, Irene. I didn't pick this house at random. I was assigned by a man – my age – to come here."

"What on earth are you on about! What man?" She was slightly angered by what she'd heard.

"Let me start at the beginning; when this man was born he was adopted legally at birth. It wasn't until he was about to be married that he was told that he wasn't their son. They told him he had the right to know. He said he loved them as his mum and dad and always would, it made no difference. After a time, he felt he'd like to know a little of his real parents without causing them any harm to their relationships with others. Apparently, his real mother was already married, and her husband was away for about a year. In that time my client was told she had a one-night stand and had to get rid of the baby before her husband returned home. If I found that the true mother was on her own with no living family, it might have been possible to meet up. If there were family, then to leave well alone. No intention would there be to cause unnecessary upheaval. I can assure you, that her family will never be contacted or told of anything. You have my word and complete assurance. I know from my investigation, that you are his mother." Marc finished his story and looked at the ashen face of Mrs Mathews. He was uneasy of what reaction to expect. He was dreading what she would do or say, his revelation came out so bluntly. Would she slap his face and tell him to get lost...

Unexpectedly, she was not hostile, she spoke calmly. "Of course you are right, you are remarkably good at your job – too damned good. But thank my son that my life will not be ruined because of it. Tell him I am deeply sorry that I could not have brought him up as my own. I'd have ruined the lives of my husband and daughter. I was ashamed of what I did, and to give away the baby was the choice I had to make. I'd betrayed my husband's trust. I got the memory of this part of my life blanked out many years ago until now, and it hurts."

Marc felt awkward, "I will shortly leave you in peace and get underway, but please could you tell me the name of his father and what he did for a living. There will be no contact made, that is a promise, your son would just like to know that much about him."

"Believe it or not I know very little about him. I can tell you his name, George Sanford – I'll never forget that name. When we met, he was working on an oil platform in the North Sea, he was on leave. He was good-looking and full of charm, I wish I'd never gone to that bloody dance that night."

Marc grabbed his suitcase and started making his way to the front door. There were so many more questions he wanted to ask but thought best not to. He didn't think George Sanford ever knew she was pregnant.

Mrs Mathews walked with him to his car.

"I will not contact you again but if ever you need me for anything, you have my address. My home phone number is in the book. Thank you for being so frank, honest and understanding," Marc said sincerely. "You've made my visit truly worthwhile."

She gave him a hug and kissed him on the cheek. She stayed and watched his car disappear out of sight at the end of the road. She had genuine tears running down her face. It hit her hard to suddenly realise that Marc was her son, seen through all of the deception that the client he had spoken of, was actually himself.

* * *

Waterford Canal

It was a beautiful day. A clear blue sky, except for a cluster of woolly clouds bunched together in the distance, resembling a flock of sheep. Waterford canal had wooden park bench seats, regularly placed along its walkway. Alan Rowland sat contentedly on one of the benches, feeding the pigeons with the last of his sandwiches.

Alan Rowland, enjoying his retirement, glanced at a younger man in an electric wheelchair not far from where he sat, who had been feeding the swans to their satisfaction. He looked at him with compassion. The younger man headed in his direction. When the man reached him, Alan said, "Good morning, nice to see someone caring for our feathered friends. I've still some tea in my flask, would you like a cup?"

"That would be nice, thank you," the other replied.

"I'm Alan," he said, handing him the freshly poured tea.

"Appreciated, I could do with that – call me Ted." He sipped the tea. "Any sugar?" he politely asked.

Alan unscrewed a jar of sugar and gave it to Ted with a teaspoon. Ted put one spoonful in the tea, stirred it in and drank half of the contents.

Alan would have liked to have asked about his disability, but thought it not quite the thing to do. Some found it extremely patronising to be asked such questions.

"Mankind could not exist without animals, you know, and yet they are very often ill-treated, it's inconceivable that anyone should want to do such things," Alan said passionately, changing his line of thought. "They supply us with milk, cheese, butter, wool, eggs, meat and much more. Guide dogs for the blind, dogs that sniff out illegal drugs and search for people under rubble whenever there's an earthquake. They are truly our friends and companions.

Then of course people race horses and dogs for money and entertainment. It greaves me to think of all the cruelty that I hear about. I always give what I can to animal charities. The animal sanctuaries have a hard time keeping open. They do such a fine compassionate service."

Ted looked at him deep in thought but did not comment immediately. Then he said after the pause, "There is a perfectly good saying, 'do unto others as you wish them to do unto you.' But since the arrival of the suicide bomber, that saying is up the creek. They do unto others as they do unto themselves."

Alan sighed and puckered his lips. "That's quite a contradiction, Ted. I've never thought of it that way before. Personally, thank goodness, I am at peace with myself. I have enough money coming in with my company and state pensions, I need no more and I'm not jealous of anyone. I do the lottery – not for myself. If I ever win the millions it would go to start a fund that would be named 'Animals in need'. Some of these top footballers earn in one week what would take me ten years to receive. I'm still in hope that some of these celebrities will start an 'Animals in need' fund some day, as they do for 'Children in need'." Alan stopped talking and watched a passing barge go slowly by.

Ted said, "You are kind-hearted, I can tell, not like the man I once knew that was entirely the opposite. A while back now, he was on the way to a group of like-minded people, for a Grouse shoot – he had no feelings or remorse for the things he did. That particular day, he was driving along a road with quite a drop on one side, with massively large trees. His front left tyre burst and the car sped over the edge spinning like a top. Always pompous and arrogant, he wore no seat belt and drove too fast – that is, when the police were not about. To begin with, he was thrown around inside of the car; the door, bonnet and boot were struck by large branches and were torn open. Somehow he found himself headfirst and halfway in the boot of the car. As the car spun, a thick branch forced the lid down on his back with tremendous force, causing serious injury to his spine. It all happened so quickly."

Another barge came along, this time those on board smiled and waved in a friendly manner. Alan and Ted waved back at them.

"As I was saying," continued Ted, "the action was just like a mouse trap. There he was, in terrible pain and unable to move, trapped by the boot lid. Then came the delirium... a mouse talking to him. 'Now you know what it feels like.' He felt the pain of the rabbit that had lead pellets shot in it, that had to crawl away and die in agony. The terrible fear of the fox that had run for miles to exhaustion, until the pack of hounds caught up with it, and tore its throat apart. The feeling of the pheasant that was blasted from the sky. And lastly before he went into unconsciousness, the taunting of a giant crab and a lobster, crushing his fingers with their claws and pincers. Then came the strong smell of petrol. 'If this car bursts into flame you will know what it is like to be cooked alive, just like we were,' they sneered menacingly. The pain and the power of the hallucination had a lasting effect, and he thereafter amended his ways. Fortunately some other motorist saw the car go over the edge and phoned for an ambulance and fire brigade on their mobile phone. The car never caught fire. If it had, he would not be alive today. That's what one of the fire crew had told him."

Alan looked at Ted. "You knew this man well then, by the sound of it. He must have done some repulsive things in his time to feel so guilty."

Ted said, "That man – I am sorry to say, was me – I am no longer that man and he deserved everything he got, that's why you find me in this chair. You may find that hard to believe what I am saying, but it's true. There's no excuse or justification for unnecessarily inflicting pain and suffering on any living creature. Unfortunately, animal abuse will go on all the time; those dishing it out are not on the receiving end. I've often wondered whether a burglar would change his ways, if his home was burgled and all of his valued personal possessions were stolen and never seen again."

With that, he drank the last of the tea and handed back the empty cup. "Thank you for your kindness," Ted said, avoiding Alan's eye contact. He then pressed the lever on his wheelchair and gradually moved away.

* * *

www.ingramcontent.com/pod-product-compliance
Lightning Source LLC
Chambersburg PA
CBHW060429260626
47161CB00005B/1845